THE SEVEN BEASTS

THE SEVEN BEASTS

SHEHZOR MUJTHEDI

PARTRIDGE

A Penguin Random House Company

To order additional copies of this book, contact
Partridge India
000 800 10062 62
orders.india@partridgepublishing.com

www.partridgepublishing.com/india

CONTENTS

CHARACTERS INTRODUCTION

King Ultimox Draco: - He is a maroon Dragon, with golden flesh crown. And he is the main protagonist of our story. He has canines pointing out of his mouth. He has got strong legs and short arms with wings on his back.

Volinoir Draco: - He is another maroon Dragon, of old age with a lot of wrinkles. He is the father of our main Protagonist. He has got the same features of the protagonist except for the crown.

Dunhardol Dorgard: - He is a Blue slim old Dragon with no wings but pointed canines. He is the detective and an informant of their castle.

Koonan: - He is our first beast in the 7 beasts. He is a snow monster beast. He is as big as a two storey building and looks like a yeti.

Troopy and Croopy: - They are the second and third beasts. They are tree beasts. They look like banyan trees. They walk on their roots.

Kampon: - He is the fourth beast. He is a chameleon beast. He is a chameleon the size of a wombat.

Kampon's 3 Brothers: - They are the 5th, 6th and 7th Beasts. They are the brothers of Kampon. They match all his features except for that they cannot talk.

PROLOGUE

Kings are not born, they are made. This quotation is very much useful and logical in our world, but only within our world. Only till the reach of humans. There are a lot of humans who believe in extraterrestrial life. They say that, there are creatures named aliens living thousands of lightyears away from our earth. They portray them with big oval eyes, huge skulls and green skin. I agree with the part that there is extraterrestrial life living somewhere far off in another world. But what kind of portraying is that? What if aliens are not something that looks way too strange like that? Today, I am revealing the secret of the extraterrestrial life. My friends, there are aliens, but they are not the way we think they are.

They are mythical beasts. They don't exist in our world, but in a far off other planet. The legends of the mythical creatures started when they sometimes came in our world through the portal door. The portal door was a small door somewhere in some grassy mountains, that door connected our world from there's. There are many kinds of mythical creatures over there, from the fierce dragons, to gentle mermaids. They know about our existence, where we live, and what we are.

We talk about them, as stories with no existence. We search them on our own world but don't realize that they come here only once in a blue moon, mostly by accident.

They think of us the same way we think of them, dangerous, ruthless and barbaric creatures with no mercy.

So let's talk about the planet and them. Their planet is called Sedcas, (Name of a beast god). It was approximately the size of our moon. It didn't have any continents, only countries. There were like about 8 countries, Lon Capturite, Derek Mohaun Foreste, Frostey snowland, Wimber Grasslands, Farme, Woodrust, Delewarete and the biggest country Beast Lande. During the medieval times, like the 4500s of Sedcas and 1400s of Earth, the planet was very old but still it had no idea about electricity. Everything was like the 11th century. There was a dynasty of Dragons, Called the Draco dynasty. It started during the 3900s of Sedcas. This dynasty didn't need to quarrel over which son should be the king. Over there, Kings were not made, they were born. The son which had to be the king was born with a crown on their head. All the other sons were made the ministers and the daughters were made the maids but were released after the daughter's marriage. The crown looked like a group of horns but it was flesh. When the dragon was about 100 years old, the crown would fall off his head. That time, the son who would be about 40-50 years (Which is like a really young age for them) would be made the king. He would rule until his crown falls off and his son would be made the next king. During the 4400s, the king Lon Descretes Evenisor Volinoir Draco's (Also called Volinoir Draco) crown fell off. He had twelve sons and six daughters, all of them unmarried. The son with the crown was named Lon Descretes Velinzer Ultimox Draco. He was made the king when his father's crown fell off at the age of 103 when Ultimox was 44 years old. He had been made the king right after the crown falling of his father.

He had been ruling as a great king all these years. But when he was around 63 years of age, he got news from his detective that the king of Lon Capturite is planning to attack on beastlande with a really huge and powerful army. This was the first time Ultimox Draco had to fight a war because there was mostly peace over there. So he asked his detective for some advice. The detective said that among all these powerful beasts on this planet, there are 7 beasts more powerful than any other beast on this planet, each having their own special power. Draco was really happy on listening this. He ordered his army to get ready to leave, in the search of the 7 beasts.

CHAPTER 1

SEARCHING FOR THE BEASTS

The day had begun like any other normal day in Beast Lande. King Ultimox Draco was sitting on his throne. The court was empty except for his ministers and maids. "My detective is late today", he said to himself. His detective, informant and advisor, Dorgard was an old dragon who had been serving the kingdom from the past 400 years.

On this day, he had come a little late. He had come nearly an hour after the time. He walked to the king with his old stumpy feet. "Dorgard!" King Draco said, "You've finally arrived. What took you so long today?" The detective spoke in his old voice, "forgive me your majesty. But the news I have found today is more important than anything else". King Draco questioned with a doubtful face, "And... What is it?" "Your majesty, the king of Lon Capturite is planning for a war. And his army is of a thousand strong beasts", the detective answered fearfully. "War?" King Draco cried with shock, "I have never fought a war before. I don't even know how to fight a war. We all lived so peacefully and we both were really friendly countries. So why did he suddenly plan for a war?" Dorgard replied, "I am, but an informant your majesty. But I don't know anyone's personal thoughts. Sadly I can't read minds". This news left King Draco stunned and shocked. He couldn't make a decision, and there was no option except to fight and lose. "Dorgard, you are old and experienced, please give me some advice", King Draco asked his detective in hope for some solution. The detective thought for a while and finally spoke, "Your majesty, There is a solution to it. But this task is considered impossible". "Tell it to me then", King Draco exclaimed, "At least there is a chance. Nothing is lost in trying". Dorgard took a deep breath and spoke, "This task is simple, just a treasure hunting game. The difference is that, this is the hardest treasure hunting game on this planet. But the treasure is also worth the search. The treasure is not one, but 7. The treasure is the 7 beasts. Among all the beasts on this planet, there are 7 beasts, more powerful than any other beast, each having their own special quality. But to find them is more difficult than touching the moon. Many famous adventurers have tried finding them, but had miserably failed. They claimed these 7 beasts to be just a story and quit the search. I won't ask you not to search. You should try at least. So don't give up your search". Draco said, "I will find them for sure, but first I need to talk to my father". The detective said, "Be quick your majesty. The war will begin within a month".

Draco walked upstairs to his father's room. He knocked on the door. He slowly peaked in and saw his father sitting on his bed. "Dad", Draco said, "I really need to talk to you". His father looked at him and said, "Ultimox, what has happened that you are here. You look nervous, and I can see some fear in your eyes". Ultimox said in a sad voice, "Dad, we are under attack, the king of Lon Capturite is planning for a war. And his army is really big and strong. There is only one way we can stop this. My detective has told me that on this planet there are 7 beasts more powerful than any other beast on this planet. So I have to begin my quest to find them, I have to go and return as fast as I can. But I need your permission before I leave". His father thought for some time and said, "The 7 Beasts? I know about that story, I don't think they really exist, but as it is the only way we can survive, I give you leave to go". They hugged each other and Ultimox left the room. He ordered his soldiers to get ready to begin the search.

They left to search for the beasts the next day. They shipped all over the planet. First, they started their search in the Frostey Snowland. They searched all over that place but didn't find anything that even looked like a beast except for giant polar bears and flying penguins. A soldier asked, "Your Majesty, we are searching for these beasts for the past 5 hours but we didn't find any". Draco said in an angry voice, "Maybe, we can find the Beasts, if you people just, OPEN YOUR EYES!! Now split up in different directions, and find the beasts, even if it costs your life".

The soldiers split up in different directions. "Grumpy King", whispered one soldier to himself. The soldier was with a few other soldiers. He said to them, "Don't you think the king is a little angry today?" Another soldier said, "Who knows, maybe he is scared of losing the battle so he is putting the pressure on us". The soldiers kept walking for some time, until one soldier said, "Hey wait a minute, why does the ground feels like skin of a beast". The other soldier said, "There is only one way to know". He started stamping the ground and said all the others do to it. They all stamped the ground together.

Suddenly, a huge snow monster got up from there. He had white fur and dark blue skin with a blue face that looked like a chimpanzee with big nose. He had an angry expression on his face. He had big and sharp teeth. "I AM HUNGRY!!!" It cried, "I AM GONNA EAT YOU ALL!!!!" A soldier said, "I can't believe my eyes. Is it really one of the 7 beasts?" Another soldier screamed to the beast, "Listen to me! Are you one of the 7 beasts?" The beast cried, "Yes! I am Koonan, The snow monster beast. And I am hungry!! I am going to eat you all!!!!" The soldier said, "If you come with us, we will take care of you for the rest of your life!!!" The beast said, "If that's the case, then take me with you people, but don't you dare fool me, for I can eat any person I want and soon you will be over".

They had taken Koonan to Draco and they had made the deal. Draco was really happy with this. But still they had to find 6 more beasts. The next place they went to was Derek Mohaun forests.

Over there, it took longer than the first time. They were wandering in the forest from nearly 2 days but could not find anything. Draco had again ordered the soldiers to split up. But still there was no sign of a beast. After about 3 hours, of search, a group of soldiers reached at the edge of the Derek Mohaun Forest. Near the Poisonous Sea. A soldier said, "Forget this, I don't want to waste my time anymore. We have searched the whole forest but did not find anything". Suddenly a voice came from behind, "stop making noise, I am trying to sleep". They looked behind but nothing was there. "Who's there?" a soldier questioned. "Can't you see me, I am right here". The voice came from a tree. Suddenly they noticed that there were two big banyan trees with a face. A soldier asked, "Wait a minute, are you both a part of the 7 beasts?" They nodded. The soldier said, "I thought that the word beast is used for animals, not for trees like you". One of the trees said, "I am Troopy, and this is my brother Croopy, and we both are the tree beasts. We are the only trees that can walk and suddenly blend in between trees. But living here is very hard for us as the rainfall here is very low and the sea right in front of us is poisonous". The soldier said, "If you come with us, then we will give you both a new home with a lot of water". They agreed to go with them.

Draco was really happy on knowing that two more beasts have been found. It was not as hard as he thought. But now it was getting harder. They kept on searching for 2 weeks but could not find any more beasts. They searched all over the planet. Even in Lon Capturite with a disguise, but failed.

They returned to Beast Lande and just then, Draco remembered that they had searched all over the planet except in their own kingdom. Draco had ordered all the homes to be emptied for one day. They searched in all the houses but didn't find any beast. Draco was really upset with this. He went out for a walk in the forest of his kingdom. Over there, he saw a small hut, the size of a living room. He went in there and saw, it was completely empty, except that there was one chair in the middle. He went and sat on the chair and thought about the good times, which were about to end. Suddenly, he noticed that he was not sitting on the chair; he was sitting on the air. Something was there, something invisible. Draco heard a voice crying, "MOVE FROM ME!!" Draco jumped out of the chair. He saw something on it; it was a big chameleon, of like 2 feet long. It looked at Draco and said, "Oh no, King Ultimox Draco, I am sorry for shouting on you. But hello, I am Kampon the Chameleon beast". King Draco looked at him with a smile and said, "So you are also one of the 7 beasts?" He nodded. King Draco said, "Good, I have found 4 of the beasts, now I have to find just 3 more. Can you tell me where are they?"

Kampon said, "I know them very well, they are my three brothers with nearly the same powers as much as me. But they are unnamed. So it is hard to differentiate them. And yeah, they are inside the poisonous sea". King Draco went with him to the poisonous sea.

At the poisonous sea, Kampon made a horn like noise through his mouth. All 3 Chameleon beasts came out of the water. King Draco jumped in joy as he had found all the 7 beasts.

On the day of the battle, the seven beasts took the lead in fighting and the king was the commander. And guess who won the battle? Who had to win? It was King Ultimox Draco who won. Now the Beasts lived with him. This was the first time King Ultimox Draco had fought a war, and also it was the first battle he won. They didn't have to fight much. The king of Lon Capturite on seeing the power of the beasts had surrendered himself. This was the first time in history that a king had won his first battle. As they had made a history, the King had made a celebration. He had put a fiesta in his palace, for all the citizens of Beast Lande. It was the best day in his life.

CHAPTER 2

FLOOD AWAY

After the great fiesta, the 7 beasts were given their own rooms. The 3 unnamed chameleon beasts were tried to be given names but it was of no use, because they couldn't talk and they were identical triplets who were impossible to differentiate. Those 3 had to share one room. Koonan was really big; he was the size of a two storey building. He couldn't fit through the doors, so he was given place inside the court. That night, all of them slept peacefully without any knowledge about what would happen the next day.

The next day, everyone woke up with a happy face, and a good mood. King Draco was always the first one to get up during the morning. He walked out to his balcony to watch the view from there. He would do that every morning. But this morning it was different. He could smell water. He looked down and saw, a flood had destroyed the city. He ran down stairs shouting, "BEASTS!!! GET READY!! WE HAVE SOME WORK TO DO!!!" All the beasts came out and they all ran outside. They saw the whole city was flooded with water, 6 feet deep. Draco said, "What happened last night?" Croopy said, "of course, a flood". Draco said, "I know but how?"

Croopy said, "We need to ask someone who was awake at late night". Everyone looked at Koonan as they all knew he was awoken till late night. Koonan said, "okay I admit it I was wake up till late night because I don't sleep a lot. At like 2 'o' clock in the night, I could smell water outside. I was feeling sleepy so I ignored it". Draco said, "now what shall we do of this?" Troopy said, "Wait a minute, I can make myself of some use, Lets absorb all this Croopy". Croopy said, "But Troopy, this is a lot of water, we cannot absorb it all". Troopy said, "Let's do at least how much we can".

They both stood in the water and started absorbing it. Draco said to himself, "This is not going to work. I need to do something". Suddenly, an idea struck his mind. "Hey Koonan", He said, "Let us both dig a hole and drain all the water into it. By that time, Troopy and Croopy, you both keep the water in control. And Dorgard, Kampon and his brothers, all of you help the citizens get out of their houses and bring them in the palace".

Everyone did as instructed while Draco and Koonan were digging the hole. After 3 hours, the whole water was drained in the hole. The citizens were returned to their home. The source of the flood was found to be coming from north direction. They constructed a small barrier in that direction.

That night they slept peacefully with the hope that the next day should go better. But who has seen the future.

The next day Draco got up and walked out to the balcony as usual. Today again, he could smell that water. He looked down and saw the flood, again. "Not again", He said to himself. He ran downstairs calling the beasts. All of them ran outside and looked at the flood. Draco said, "But we had constructed a dam, what happened to it?" Everyone looked at Koonan again. He said nervously, "What could I do? I was hungry. I didn't eat anything the whole day and I worked really hard. So that was the only thing I found capable of eating". Draco gave himself a facepalm and said, "Oh Koonan. Forget it anyways. Whatever, we will do what we did yesterday". They all again did their duties and after a few hours, everything was okay again. Because of this flood the king was getting really less time for managing the court.

This night, Koonan was locked inside a cage. They slept somewhat peacefully. The next morning, what would happen? It happened what was happening since two days. There was a flood again. And like every day the King said, not again. This day, they noticed that koonan was out of the cage. The cage was also not there. King Draco stared into Koonan's eyes with anger and said, "How did you do this?" Koonan replied with a little fear, "What do you think? The one who ate a dam couldn't eat a cage?" This time King Draco was really angry. He told Koonan that if he ate anything once more, then he would be thrown from his kingdom. They repaired everything drained the water and it was how their day went again.

The next day, guess what happened? The kingdom was flooded again, but this time it was not Koonan.

King Draco looked at Koonan again and said, "TELL ME THE TRUTH!!!!!" Koonan cried with fear, "I swear it!! I didn't do anything today!!!" They all went to see what had happened to the dam. They saw that the dam was broken by the pressure of the flood. They tracked the direction, to find out from where the water was coming. They found out that it was coming from Delewarete, The north pole of Sedcas. Draco and the 7 beasts, planned to go there.

The next day, when they reached to Delewarete, Draco said, "Everyone split up once more, in different directions and look for something suspicious".

Everyone did as Draco asked them to. They split up in different directions in search of something suspicious which could be the root of the entire problem. They searched for a lot of time. At the end, Draco found a big hole in the ground. "Everyone! Come here!" he screamed. Everyone reached there and looked at that hole. "What is this?" Koonan asked. Draco said, "there is only one way to know", and he jumped in that hole. All of them were surprised by that. Kampon asked, "What shall we do now?" Koonan said, "Let's just do what he did," saying this, he too jumped in. All the other beasts followed him and jumped in.

CHAPTER 3

DOWNTOWN OF DINOSAURS

"Where are we falling!!??" Koonan asked while falling into the hole. Kampon answered, "How are we supposed to know? It was your idea to jump in". Koonan replied, "It was not my idea, it was Draco who jumped in first. Wait a minute, where is Draco?" A voice came from really down, "I am here, I am still falling, this pit is really deep!!!" After a long time, they heard a loud noise. They heard Draco say, "I've finally reached down here".

After some time they also reached to the bottom of the pit, they fell from a great height but still, they did not feel any pain, as beasts are used to it. They met Draco down there. The pit was so deep that it took them nearly 5 minutes to fall till the bottom of the pit.

"Okay, now what next?" Koonan asked. Draco said, "You must be blind. Can't you see that big hole over there on your right side. Koonan looked at his right side and said, "It is not a hole, it looks like a passage. And I can see light coming through it, let's go in there". Draco went in the passageway first and all the others followed him.

At the end of the passageway, they could see light Draco looked out from there and cried out, "Everyone! Come here, fast". They all looked outside and they saw, guess what they saw? They saw that under the ground, there was another town. That town had its own underground sun, and it had many small houses and straight in the middle, there was a big castle made up of bricks.

When they went inside the town, they got their second surprise; the town was full of big scaly lizards with sharp teeth and powerful bodies. Draco went over and asked to one of them, "Excuse me, what are you people?" That one was of green colour and was a little shorter than Draco, he had a big face and massive body and long claws. "What kind of question is that?" he said, "I need to ask you the same question". Draco said, "I am King Ultimox Draco, A dragon of the Draco dynasty of beastlande, and these are my seven beasts". The other beast said, "Oh so you are King Ultimox Draco, please come to my house so we can talk with peace".

Draco and the 7 beasts went to his house, Koonan couldn't fit in through the door so lifted the roof up and went in. The beast gave them all some things to eat. Draco asked, "What is this?" The beast said, "This is called a fish, it is an aquatic animal. It is really delicious and healthy, try it please". Draco and the 7 beasts ate it and couldn't resist taking more. After some time, the beast said, "So let me introduce myself, I am Dipord, a Dinosaur". Draco interrupted, "What's a Dinosaur?" Dipord said, "Dinosaurs were big creatures which lived on the planet earth. But nearly 65 million years ago, the food had finished over there, so we had come to this planet through a door we found in the grasslands. But we couldn't adjust with the beasts on this planet so we made our own town with an artificial sun. But as the town is very small, our population also has to be very less, so we have a one child policy and death penalty even for a small crime. Our king is very heartless and he loves to kill little dinosaurs. If anyone has got twins or triplets, he orders the extra babies to be killed. This king deserves to die himself". King Draco said, "I need to talk to this king right now". Dipord said, "Thank you sir but I don't think that this king will listen to you". King Draco said, "He has to listen, that's the only way he can live".

They went to his court. Dipord said to the king, "Your majesty, the king of Beast Lande has come here to meet you". The king said, "What does he wants to talk with me? With king Undord The Great?" Dipord said, "I don't know about that Sire, but will you please talk to him?" The king said, "If he disappoints me, then he will be executed, but for now, send him in!" King Draco walked in with his seven beasts, "Good morning King Undord". The king interrupted and cried out, "You have disappointed me in the beginning. Is that how you address the great king? You foolish person". King Draco said, "You didn't even deserve that. I gave you way more than you deserved. You are supposed to be addressed as, bad morning foolish and heartless 'king'!!" The king's face turned red with anger and he shouted, "WHAT HAVE I DONE WRONG?" Draco replied normally, as if he didn't feel his tone, "You killed innocent baby dinosaurs, separated them from their mothers. And you killed small thieves also who had done nothing but stole some food from a shop because he was hungry. Does that not make you heartless?" The king was even angrier now and he shouted again, "I DID THAT FOR THE BENEFIT OF MY KINGDOM AND MY PEOPLE!!" Draco replied with the same tone as before, "No, You killed these people not because you should, but because you could, you killed them because you loved seeing them die. You killed them because you had the power to, you killed them because no one had the power or courage to stop you, but not anymore, this ends today, and you are going to stop this at once!!" This time the king was angrier than a devil, his face turned red as blood. He shouted with full anger, "ENOUGH!!!! SOLDIERS!!!! ARREST THESE FOOLS WHO HAVE NO RESPECT FOR THE KING!!!" Draco said in a relaxed voice, "No they can't!!!" Saying this, he spit huge fireballs on the guards who were trying to arrest him. Koonan froze them with his icy breath, troopy and croopy bruised them with their thorns and Kampon and his brothers gave them stealth attacks by disappearing and hitting them with their tongues. At the end, all the soldiers surrendered, and the king did surrender as well and he had sworn not to kill any more babies or thieves. Draco had given order that all the dinosaurs from now on wards will live in Beast Lande. While leaving, Draco asked Dipord, "Listen Dipord, I am thankful to help you but will you please help me clear one doubt. There is a flood going on in Beast Lande since 3 days, do you know where is it coming from?" Dipord answered, "I know the place, it is near this place only, There is a cave which has a blue cauldron in it, That cauldron creates water once in 300 years, so that water flows and goes all the way to BeastLande, this flood comes once in 300 years for 1 full year. If you want to stop it, you need to destroy the cauldron. It can be destroyed only by fire, you should try doing it". They waved their good bye and Draco and his 7 beasts went out of the pit. Draco said, "The cave must be nearby somewhere so let's search for it. Koonan said, "No need to search for it, It's just over there". Draco said, "Oh yeah, you people wait outside for me, I will come out in sometime".

Draco went into the cave and walked further inside. Soon he saw bright blue light shining out of a blue cauldron. Draco said, "So you sir, are the reason for all the floods in my place. Don't worry, you will rest in peace, in a better place". Saying this Draco blew fire all over it and in a few seconds, the cauldron blasted but Draco had run away by that time.

CHAPTER 4

A NEW INTRUDER

It was during the night time. King Ultimox Draco was sleeping in peace, just then, he woke up in the middle of the night. He was being disturbed by noises of horses running around. He looked out of the window and he saw, A unicorn, but not those cute unicorns which we know. He saw a black unicorn with red eyes, His eyes were not looking forward, they were looking straight at draco. He was hidden in the darkness of the night. He could be seen only through his red eyes. He looked really creepy. Draco ignored it and went back to sleep.

The next morning he woke up normally and like every morning he went out to the balcony and looked out at his kingdom. He went back to his room and downstairs to have his breakfast, the day went normally like every other day.

That night, Koonan had suddenly woke up in the middle of the night. He was being disturbed by noises of horses running out. He went and saw a black unicorn with red eyes, the same which Draco had seen last night. Koonan ignored it too and went to sleep.

The next day also went normally. But at the night, this time troopy had seen the unicorn. And the next night Croopy had seen it, and after that Kampon had seen it and after that, Kampon's three brothers had seen it.

The next night, Dorgard was sleeping in his room. Just then he woke up, he looked out and saw that black unicorn. The unicorn's red eyes had striked fear into the eyes of Dorgard. Dorgard did his prayers and slept silently.

The next morning during the breakfast, Dorgard suddenly asked, "has anyone seen a black unicorn with red eyes during his sleep?" "Yes I have", everyone said at once. "Oh no", Dorgard said, "I think the unicorn is some sort of evil spirit. It is spying on us and soon it will consume all of our souls". Draco said, "Nonsense, it must be our hallucination or a dream". Dorgard said, "So everyone has got the same hallucination or dream?" Draco's father said, "I had also seen this unicorn when I was around 65 years old". The detective said, "We can't hold on anymore, this night we all must look for that unicorn and catch it".

That night, they all were outside, hidden in the environment. Draco was hidden in some bushes, Koonan was lying down next to the boundary of the castle. Troopy and Croopy hid as trees. Kampon and his brothers became invisible. That night, they saw the unicorn running around. Suddenly, Draco flew out of the bushes and chased the unicorn and caught it.

They took it inside the court and interrogated it. A few soldiers were holding its legs while Draco was questioning him. "Tell me! Who are you?" Draco questioned. "Your enemy. Your terrible death. That's what I am", It said. Draco got really angry and scratched his neck. Some blood oozed out from the cut and fell to the ground. Draco asked again, "This might have knocked some sense into your mind. Now tell me, who are you?" This time, the unicorn was really angry. It spit on Draco's face and kicked the soldiers who were holding him and ran away from there.

Draco chased it for a long time but soon, it disappeared into the darkness. Draco went back to his castle with an angry mood.

He was angry more than anything. This was the first time someone had spit on his face.

He went to his room and slept that night with anger. The beasts couldn't do anything. They could just hope that by the next morning he will be cooled down. But they could just hope.

Even the next morning, Draco was still angry. He couldn't get out of his angry mood. He was arrogant on the on the breakfast table. He didn't want to talk to anyone.

After the breakfast, he went to his room and slammed the door. His father was not happy with his behavior.

He went to his room and knocked on his door, "Draco", He said, "Open the door my son. We have to find that unicorn". Draco opened the door and said, "Oh father, it's you. Okay come in". Draco's father was with him in the room. His father said, "You know son. You have no rights to be so angry on such a small thing". Draco interrupted, "Such a small thing? He spat on my face, the face of the king of this place. How dare he do that?" his father said, "It's not a big deal, Not at all. You should ignore such kind of people. But I really wonder who he was". Draco said, "We need to find that out, Somehow".

They went downstairs. There they got the news that all the dinosaurs have shifted to Beast lande, but the king has suddenly died for no reason. Draco thought of it to be strange. Maybe it was a co incident. Or maybe it was a conspiracy. What could it actually be? A sudden death for no reason, really?

But that was not King Ultimox Draco's problem. His problem was, what was that unicorn, who was he. Why was he coming there? And he called himself the king's greatest enemy. What did it mean? Did he really mean it? There are many questions, but to find the answers, we need to keep on moving.

CHAPTER 5

THE SEARCH FOR AN ENEMY

King Draco was surprised by listening to the news of the death of king. It seems that the king had died just an hour after they left. During that time, King Draco was inside the cave. But now he doesn't has time to investigate about who's dead, but it's about to find out who is alive. And where is he.

After a few days, King Ultimox Draco was sleeping during the night. Just then, he heard the voice, the voice which made him go angry, the voice which made him suspicious, the voice which made him confused, the voice of the Unicorn running.

He looked out of the window. And saw that unicorn, again. And he felt that anger, again. He opened the window and jumped out and flew after the unicorn. The unicorn was really fast this time, running faster than the wind. But Draco wasn't slow either. They both were really tired but couldn't stop, each because of their own reasons, one for revenge, and other for survival. The unicorn slowly disappeared into the darkness. Draco quickly landed down into the darkness. He couldn't lose him this time. He looked around in the darkness searching for him, just then, he felt a really hard kick on his face, and then everything went black.

When he woke up, he found himself in a dark room, which had a small lamp in the middle which gave some light. Draco Breathe fire around there which made the room a little bit visible, He saw that the room was totally closed except for a door, Draco walked to the door and tried to open it but it was locked from outside. All he needed to open the door was just spitting fire on it. That's what he did and the whole door had melted. Draco walked out and he found himself in Beast Lande, Somewhere far away from his Castle. He flew up in the sky to get a better view.

He saw that he was like 20 kilometers away from his castle. He flew there to his castle.

At his castle, everyone was happy to see him. All of them asked him where was he all the time. He said, "I don't know. Last night I had seen that unicorn again. I chased him all the way into the darkness. He kicked on my face really hard and I dropped unconscious. When I woke up I found myself in a small hut with a metal door. I melted it and flew away from, there to here". Dorgard said, "Your Majesty, Will you please take me to that hut". Draco took him there.

The detective searched the room for clues. He examined the lamp closely and said, "Your majesty this lamp is not anything normal, it is a lamp which doesn't need oil to work, I don't know how it works, but it must be very innovative, and this is maybe a clue to us. Sir, will you please blow fire into it". Draco did as he was said. The detective went out and said, "Sir this lamp is glowing brighter when faced to one direction. You have to follow its trail and it may lead you to something big". Draco said, "Thanks for your help Dorgard, now I must leave you back to the castle".

Draco left Dorgard at the castle and then he begun with his search.

He continued searching for the unicorn. He followed the directions which the lamp directed him. The lamp directed him inside a forest. He walked through the trees and bushes. Now the lamp guided him to climb a mountain. Draco climbed it. Now the lamp guided him to go inside a cave of the mountain. Draco walked in the cave.

The cave was really dark and empty except for the light the lamp was giving. The sound of Draco's footsteps echoed within the cave. He walked until he discovered another cauldron inside the cave, this cauldron was brown in color and it gave out greenish brown light.

"Now what is this thing?" Draco said. He walked around the cauldron as he inspected it. "Maybe if I destroy this", He said to himself, "Another big problem may be solved". Draco breathe fire on it and ran away from the cave before the cauldron blasted.

He returned back to the castle. He said to everyone about the second cauldron.

That night, he was half asleep and half awake. He was waiting for the unicorn to come. But all night, the sound of the unicorn, never came.

The next day, Draco woke up as usual. The day went as usual, like every other day. Even that night, no noises of the unicorn came again. The days went as usual, and the nights too. There were no sightings or sounds of the unicorn.

That black unicorn, was a great enemy of Draco whose name, history, personality, everything remained mystery. No one had ever again seen that unicorn or heard about it. Maybe it was dead, or maybe it was alive, preparing for some attack.

CHAPTER 6

THE CREEPY CAVE

King Ultimox Draco, Volinoir Draco, The 7 Beasts and Dorgard were out on a walk. Draco was in a good mood today. "Dorgard", Draco spoke suddenly, "Without a doubt. You are old and experienced, and you hold a better knowledge of Beast Lande, More than me. So, can you tell me any adventurous and mysterious place in beast lande?" Dorgard thought for a while and then replied, "Your majesty, Beast Lande is a country of peace. There are many interesting and fun places in here. But it's not important for every place to be fun. There are a few haunted and mysterious places as well. But most of these places are not really haunted, they are just mysterious, they are rumored to be haunted, but some are really haunted". "Interesting", Draco said, "Tell me the names of the places which are really haunted". Dorgard answered, "Your Majesty, There are many places which are really haunted but I don't remember where they are. I only remember one place". "What is it?" Draco asked. "The Cave of Nogletune, Your majesty", The detective said. "Then let's go there", Draco said.

They started walking in the direction which the detective told them. While walking, the detective described the cave. "The cave is as big as double the size of your castle", He said, "It is so dark that the color black would look glowing when compared to the darkness of the cave. You can listen to the sounds of nocturnal insects but you can't see them. You can feel big bats flying around. Rarely, we can listen to roars of Beastly bears and howls of powerful wolves. But no one knows if there are really bears and wolves inside. Some people say that the voice is just our imagination, our fear which makes imaginary voices. Our brain makes sounds relating to the environment. We must not fear if we listen to the sounds of any dangerous beasts". "We don't need to", Draco said. "Good then", the detective said.

After sometime, they reached to the cave. They all were standing in front of the cave. Draco said, "My god, it's emitting darkness". The detective said, "Your majesty, even if you breathe fire while within the cave. The fire will appear brighter than the sun". Draco said, "But I am not scared, neither are my beasts". Volinoir Draco said, "That's the spirit my son. Let's go in". Dorgard said, "I can't guarantee you all that we will come out alive. But it's a really big risk". Draco said, "Dorgard? Are you coming in or not?" Dorgard answered, "Of course your majesty. I am coming".

They walked into the dark cave. They could feel their heart hammering to their ribs. As if it would break open and come out. Didn't think it would be so scary. The darkness was enough to scare them. But they had their bravery and boldness in them to help them not to turn back. They were totally silent. Not even the sound of breathe. They kept walking, No turning back now, No stopping them now.

After sometime, the noises started, the noises of the bats flying. They could feel the bats flying past them. Slowly the noises increased. They could listen to the noises of the bats, eagles, wolves, bears etc. They walked as fast as they could and tried to ignore the noises.

After a lot of time, they could see light coming from a little far away. They had reached to the end point. They ran outside and fell to the ground. They took very deep breathes. "WE ARE ALIVE!!!!!" Koonan cried with joy. Kampon said, "Why were we inside, it was completely pointless to be in a creepy cave for no reason". Draco said, "No. I think I have discovered something. Inside the cave, we could listen to the noises of eagles, even though eagles don't go inside caves. They like to fly high in the sky. So how were there noises of eagles inside the cave?" Just then they saw an eagle fly out of the cave. The eagles in Sedcas were very big and had a massive body. That eagle flew up in circles around Draco, "my new prey!!" The eagle said and flew away. Draco said in a confused voice, "What was that?" Dorgard answered, "Another enemy. I don't why but your majesty; you are being searched by a lot by the enemies". Draco said, "What have I ever done to these beasts? Why are they all after me?"

Dorgard said, "We know only what we are supposed to know". Draco looked at Dorgard and said, "Dorgard, as you are my detective, I give you another job. Find someone who can give me answers to my questions". Dorgard said, "Your majesty, that's a really difficult job. I won't be able to that. I am old and unstable for this". Draco said, "Listen Dorgard, I give you three days to decide whether you will go or not". Dorgard said, "I will think about it sire, I will think about it. But wait a second, Kampon, you had 3 brothers right?" Kampon nodded. "But I can see only two of them, where is the third one?" Dorgard said. Draco said, "Maybe he is still in the cave. Oh god, first of all he is a chameleon and second he is in the dark, how can we find him?" Kampon said, "Stop worrying friends. He is right here; he is just invisible right now". All of them stopped worrying and they started laughing. Draco said, "Hey, wait a minute, this has given me an idea. Kampon, you guys can become invisible. Even an eagle's eye can't see you right?" He nodded again. "So this gives me the plan" Draco said mysteriously.

CHAPTER 7

A PERFECT PLAN

King Draco was out in his garden, on his daily walk. But he would walk in the city during his daily walks. Why was he walking in his own garden? Well that was actually his trap to catch the eagle. The eagle would surely come there to attack on Draco. Kampon and his brothers were invisible over there. When the eagle would come there, Kampon and his brothers would wrap their tongues around the eagle, and trap it.

Draco was walking around in the garden. Waiting for the eagle to come and strike so that they could strike back. Draco just walked around patiently. Just then, he heard an eagle's voice. He ignored it as if he didn't listen. He slowly looked up to see the eagle. The eagle swooped down to attack on Draco. It was about 7 feet close to Draco when suddenly, all the 4 chameleons shot out their tongues. The first chameleon wrapped his tongue around the neck of the eagle, the second chameleon wrapped his tongue around both of his legs, and the third chameleon wrapped his tongue around the eagle's beak. Kampon tied his tongue around the eagle's body. They pulled the eagle to down to earth. Draco gave him a strike by his tail. The eagle dropped to the ground, unconscious.

When it woke up, it found itself tied to the wall with a chain connected to his legs. Draco was standing in front of him. "Good morning. Little friend." Draco said. "I am not your friend", the eagle said, "Let me out of here". Draco said, "Nah, that would be too easy. First let me question you a bit. So what's your name little friend?" The eagle said, "I am not your friend. But you need to know about me so, I am Everet the eagle". Draco said, "Good, so do you know anything about the unicorn I met a few days ago?" The eagle said, "Yeah. He is Anchor the dark unicorn". Draco said, "Good, now tell me. Why do you beasts always want to attack on me?" Everet didn't say anything, he just started laughing mysteriously. His laugh slowly increased in volume and pitch. Draco scratched him once on the neck and the laugh turned into a scream. He screamed in pain. "Now what?" Draco said. Everet said in an angry voice, "I am not going to tell you. Let you do anything. Let you torture me. Let you bring hell upon Sedcas, I won't say". Draco said, "Alright, then you're no more use to me. Guards, we shall execute the prisoner tomorrow morning".

They put the eagle in their jail cells. The eagle had to be beheaded the next morning.

The next morning, Draco ordered his soldiers to bring the eagle to the execution ground, but the eagle had disappeared from the jail cell. They all begin to search for him but he was nowhere to be found. Draco ordered Dorgard to search for the eagle.

Dorgard was searching the jail cell for clues. After searching for some time, he said, "Your majesty, There are no openings or secret doors in this jail cell, but that window over there, its grills are far enough that if the eagle turns vertical then it can escape from there". Draco said, "So you mean it has escaped from that window?" Dorgard said, "Most likely but I cannot be sure". Draco said, "Okay so, Dorgard, have you made your decision?" Dorgard said, "Yes sir, I will leave within a month". Draco said, "Good but return as fast you can". Dorgard said, "But before that, your majesty, I have found a map over here which shows a path from here to another cave. What could this mean?" Draco said, "We will know that only when we get to that cave".

CHAPTER 8

THE CAVE AND THE CAULDRON

Draco set out alone to go to the cave. He followed the path which was shown to him by the map. The cave was pretty much far away from the castle. He was flying while navigating himself.

After a lot of time he reached to the cave. He was standing in front of it. After being in the darkest cave, this cave looked like it had some source of light inside. He walked into the cave which was somewhat bright. He could see that there were many inscriptions on the walls, there were designs which looked like they narrate a story.

There was a symbol of a tree, a few stick beasts throwing rocks on the tree. "This looks weird". Draco said to himself. He kept walking and there he saw another inscription. There was the beast illuminati symbol. The beast illuminati symbol had an eye inside a circle. Under the symbol, it was written, Mabel ivel struit Kampon. "Now what does this mean?" Draco again said to himself as he walked even deeper. Now he had seen another inscription on the wall. this one was a scary one of some figure standing on two legs which looked like a human wearing a black robe, his face could not be seen because of his black hood, But his eyes emitted red light, as red as blood. Draco kept walking. And then he reached to another cauldron, this cauldron was of light green color, He could see some cravings on the cauldron, written in some dead language which he could not understand. Draco breathe fire on that cauldron too and destroyed it.

He went back to the castle and said to Dorgard, "I am back. But Dorgard, I have seen some strange inscriptions inside the cave". Dorgard said, "Your majesty, I forgot to tell you one thing. Walking in the Cave of Nogletune helps our eye sight a lot. Our eye sight becomes a hundred times better. We can see normally in the dark, and we can also see things which are not visible to the naked eye". Draco said, "Maybe, there were hidden messages in the previous caves too, I am going there again".

Draco left to go to Delewarete, where they found the first cauldron. Draco was standing in front of the cave. He couldn't get in it. The opening was covered with rocks. Maybe the rocks had fallen when the first cauldron had blasted. Draco used his full power and removed the rocks from his way. He walked in the cave. The scenery didn't look the same as before. Well actually, Draco hadn't looked at the scenery before. It was really dark that time. Well actually, it was as dark as it was now, but now Draco could see in the dark. He inspected the walls to try to understand the inscriptions on it. He saw a big beast which reminded of Koonan, and a hundred stick beasts throwing rocks at him as the beast is trying to dodge. He kept on walking and again saw the beast illuminati symbol with those words written under it, "Mabel ivel struit Koonan". Draco kept walking and he again saw the portrait of the scary person wearing black robe. Draco continued to walk. Finally he reached to the cauldron, he saw that the cauldron had not been blasted, just the light had stopped coming from it. He saw that on this cauldron too, there were some words written in dead language. Not some words, there were a lot of inscriptions. As Draco had seen whatever he had to, he turned around and started walking back.

He had come out of the cave and started his journey to the second cave. He flew up in the sky to track his path. He followed the path which he navigated to reach to the cave. After a lot of time, he reached to the cave.

This cave was also covered with rocks. He removed those rocks from his way and entered the cave. He would feel déjà vu whenever he entered the cave which he had entered before but not seen. Draco walked deeper and then he saw the first inscription. There were trees which were being cut but, there were two trees which were being thrown stones at and not being cut. Draco kept walking forward and saw the beast illuminati symbol, with the words under it written, "Mabel ivel struit Troopy ol Croopy" Draco then walked further and saw the portrait of the person in black robe. Draco walked even deeper and saw the cauldron. This one was also not destroyed but it stopped giving the light. There were inscriptions on this cauldron too, just like the other cauldrons, not able to be understood". Draco walked out of that cave too and returned to his castle.

CHAPTER 9

THE SKELETON

Draco was back in his castle. He talked to Dorgard about the things he had seen inside the caves. Dorgard also didn't have an answer to his question. Dorgard had made arrangements to leave in search of answers. Dorgard was going to leave within a week. Draco wanted him to leave as fast as he could. He was really desperate for his answers.

Draco was relaxing on his throne as he had nothing to do. He started to make theories in his head about what was all this. Suddenly, he heard Dorgard shouting, "Your Majesty!! We are under attack!!!" Draco got up and asked Dorgard, "What happened?" Dorgard did not get calm; he said in the fearful voice, "There is an enormous skeleton of a big beastly lion outside. It is bigger than Koonan and cannot be stopped, please do something". Draco understood that it was a moment in which we can't calm down. He said in a loud voice, "The 7 beast! Get ready, we have a guest!!" He said as he ran out of the castle, the seven beasts followed him.

They saw the skeleton destroying the homes of the people. Draco saw its enormous size. It was as gigantic as a small mountain. The skeleton looked at Draco. They had made eye contact. "So we meet again my enemy?"

The skeleton said. Draco got really very frustrated of this and cried out, "NO!!!! NOT ANOTHER BEAST I HAVE NEVER MET CALLING ME HIS ENEMY!!!" The skeleton said, "You have been mistaken my enemy, have you forgotten all the fights we had together?" Draco felt really angry. He flew up in the sky and spitted huge fire balls on the skeleton. The skeleton tried to block it but failed. It had no other choice except to run away. It tried running away but Draco shouted, "Beasts!! Don't let it escape!!!" The 7 beasts caught it and made it unconscious.

There was no place to interrogate a beast of this size. So Draco had put it in the Beast Lake. It was a lake as big as, triple the size of the whole castle. The skeletons legs were inside the water but rest of the body was outside. They had tied his legs under water to the floor of the lake.

It woke up after a lot of time. It couldn't get out of the water as he was tied to the floor and he couldn't break the ropes because his legs couldn't apply that much force under water. Draco was right in front of it when it woke up. "Okay so, let me interrogate you like every other enemy which I have found. So tell me who are you?" The skeleton spoke, "Why don't you remember us?" Draco got really angry from his answer and spit fire on his face. The skeleton struggled in pain. Draco said, "What will you answer now?" The skeleton said, "Fine, I am not interested in dying with your hands. I am Secroop, the slave to the devil, and the enemy to the angel". Draco said, "Speak what I may be able to understand!" The skeleton said,

"I am speaking what you must understand. It's not for me to explain, but for you to understand". Draco said, "What do you mean? What does all this mean? Who are you? Who were they? Why are you all after me? Explain!" He laughed in a silent voice, mysteriously, "I have already told you", he said, "It's not for me to explain but for you to understand". This answer had left Draco in a confused situation, he couldn't understand anything. He could just pretend that he had understood, but everyone knew, he didn't understand. Draco said, "As you have said all you could, you are no more of any use to me. I give you leave to go............. To hell". Secroop got really scared on listening to this answer. He would beg for mercy but he was never taught to beg in front of his enemy. He was trapped in the water until the next morning when he would be executed by being burned alive.

The next morning, guess what happened. What could happen? Secroop had disappeared, just like the eagle. What was that, what were they? How did they disappear from a completely locked trap? Draco was really upset with this.

Draco was sitting on is throne with the palm on his face, Thinking about all the 7 beasts and those bad beasts who called him his enemy. Dorgard was standing in his place with the ministers. Draco looked at Dorgard. They both made eye contact. Suddenly, Draco got up and said, "Dorgard, you are leaving at once". Dorgard's expression suddenly changed and he said in a fearful voice, "But, your majesty what have I done?" Draco said, "I mean go and search for my answers right now". Dorgard was really scared of King Draco's anger. He said, "But sir, I can't leave suddenly, at least give me time till tomorrow". Draco said, "Okay then. I don't want to see your face after tomorrow evening". Dorgard answer, "Yes your majesty".

But before he would leave, who knew another chaos had yet to come, but this was not one of his enemies, someone, he never knew, someone.

CHAPTER 10

THE HUMAN INVASION

What was happening in another planet is a different thing; first let's learn what was happening in our world before going beyond limits. No, I am not going away from the story line. Let's see what was going on in our world during that time, During the 4500s of Sedcas, and 1400s of planet earth. Somewhere in a far off village, there was a 15 years old orphan named Drake Wimberton. He was a white blonde with blue eyes. One of his qualities was that he was really curious. As a child, he had been abused a lot by his step parents. He was still being abused, and he would be abused.

One day, he had accidentally dropped a pot of water in a hurry. His parents abused him more than a lion. This made Drake really angry. He was so angry; he ran away from his home and went into the hills.

He was crying in anger as he ran. The cool breeze cut through his body. He ran uphill, he wouldn't get tired by that, his anger was a bigger problem than feeling tired.

He kept running up hill, when suddenly, he had been tripped down by a rough rock. He fell right in front of a small door. The door was made of Oakwood and had a brass handle. The door was the size of a rabbit hole.

Drake got up and opened the door. The door emitted darkness as it opened. Drake was really angry that time. He didn't know what to do. He decided to go in that hole and be inside until he cools down. He went inside the dark hole. He was sitting upright in the hole with the door closed.

He was getting cooled down slowly, but now, curiosity got the better of him. He was feeling curious about what is there in this hole and where does it lead. He couldn't control his curiosity and went deeper inside the hole. He kept on going until he fell down. He suddenly fell down because the hole had ended. That hole was no other hole but the portal. He fell inside and now was in the galaxy. After sometime, he fell down to the other end of the portal, in Sedcas.

He was now, in the hole of Sedcas, he climbed out of there from the door on the other side. Then he opened the door and went out. He found himself, in BeastLande.

He was in the forest of beastlande. He kept walking to get to a civilized town or something. After a lot of time, he reached to the town near Draco's castle. He took a sigh of relief. But when he saw the beasts, he stopped breathing. On seeing him, the beasts gathered around him. Drake had fainted with shock and he fell to the ground.

The beasts took him to the castle of Draco. There, Draco was preparing for the leave of Dorgard. They had made arrangements for him to leave, but now, they had got the trouble of this human intruder.

Draco was sitting on his throne waiting for Dorgard to come back after waving goodbye to his family. But instead of Dorgard, his minister came there and said, "Your majesty, there is a group of citizens who claim that they have brought something to show you. Shall I send them in?" Draco said, "No, no, no, no, no, no, no, no, no, no, no!!! I don't want another enemy I have never met". The minister said, "No sir, they say they have brought something which they cannot identify". Draco said, "Okay then, send them in. Let's see what they have to show, and also, go to Dorgard's home and ask him to come faster". The minister nodded and walked out of there. The citizens came in carrying that boy. Draco looked at the boy and asked in a confused voice, "What is this?" A citizen said, "Your majesty, we found it in the town. And it fell down unconscious on seeing us all. So we have brought it to you to ask what to do with it". Draco said, "Let it be with me. You people can leave for now". The citizens bowed at Draco and left from that place.

The boy was on the floor, faint. After sometime, Dorgard came back and said, "I am sorry your majesty. I was late, my daughter had fallen sick so I had to take… care… of…. her". He started to stutter. Draco asked him, "What's the matter Dorgard?" Dorgard stammered, "Where did you get this human from?" Draco said, "Ah, just some citizens had dropped it here. Wait a minute, did you just say human?" Dorgard stammered again, "Yes it is a human". Draco said, "Holy Heavens! We need to kill it before it wakes up". Dorgard said, "No sir. It's just a small boy. I don't think it can bring any danger upon us". Draco said, "So what should we do?" Dorgard said, "First of all, we should wait for it to wake up". Draco said, "Yeah right. Let's put him in the bed of guest room". They put him on a comfortable bed of the guest room. Draco and Dorgard were standing beside the bed.

The boy woke up after a lot of time. When he woke up, he saw Draco and Dorgard towering over him. He was really scared and they could see the innocent fear in his eyes. Draco said, "Don't cry little kid. You're safe with us". Drake said in a fearful voice, "Please, I am begging you. Don't eat me". Draco said, "Don't worry, we won't eat you". Drake got up and started cry. Dorgard patted him on the back and said, "Why are you crying?" Drake said in an innocent voice, "I am scared." Dorgard said, "Why? Do you want to go home?" Drake said, "No. But because I have to go home as you people won't keep me here". Dorgard asked, "Why don't you want to go home?" Drake introduced himself and said his story about him being an orphan and how his step parents abuse him. Draco felt really emotional on listening to his story.

Draco taught him not to be afraid of the beast and they are friends and he introduced him to the 7 beasts. Dorgard's leave was postponed because of this kid coming. Dorgard trained the kid and taught him to live with the beasts.

After living nearly a month with the beasts, Drake was finally made up to some use. Secroop had attacked again at Beast Lande. Draco, 7 beasts and Drake were trying their best to stop him but now Secroop was even more powerful.

After a lot of time, Drake got an idea, "Hey Draco!" Drake cried, "Carry me high above the monster." Draco knew they didn't have time for explanation so he did as asked. Drake was on Draco's back and he flew up above Secroop. Drake jumped inside the skeleton and hanged by its ribs. He stood on its ribs and made it feel uncomfortable. He started stamping on its ribs. The skeleton left out loud painful groan. Draco and the 7 Beasts took advantage of this and started attacking on it. After sometime, the skeleton blasted. His bones scattered on the ground. They celebrated their victory, but suddenly, all the bones came together and the skeleton formed again. Secroop started running away. Draco tried to chase it, but after sometime, it disappeared into thin air. Draco went back to the town. There, he discovered a bone on the ground, He broke the bone open, and he found a map inside it. The map, showed the position, of another cauldron.

CHAPTER 11

THE FINAL CAULDRON

Draco was in his castle, he showed the map to Dorgard. Dorgard examined the map closely and said, "This map is more complicated than all the other maps. This shows the map of the who kingdom, and there are a few numbers in the top and a few numbers are highlighted. And also, there is a strange beast illuminati symbol on the right corner". Draco said, "And also, this beast illuminati symbol was there inside all the caves which I have been to". Dorgard said, "Maybe, This means that this map leads to another cave of the cauldron". Draco said, "That's not maybe, I am sure about that". Dorgard said, "Then why don't you go?" Draco said, "I am not able to understand it completely". Dorgard said, "What is not to understand in this?" Draco said, "You are right, maybe I am not able to understand where to start". Dorgard said, "You can start from here itself and follow the map". Draco said, "Okay then, I am leaving". Drake interrupted, "Wait! I too want to come with you". Draco said, "Drake, you might get injured or something". Drake said, "I don't care. I am real man, I am not scared". Draco sighed and then said, "Okay then. You never agree with me". Drake smiled and said, "Who cares, let's leave". Drake sat on the back of Draco. Draco flew up in the sky and away.

Draco navigated himself the directions. Drake hold him tight. He was feeling tickles in his stomach as they flew over a great height to a great distance.

After a lot of time, they reached to the cave. Draco landed and he put Drake on the ground. Draco asked Drake to wait outside, but Drake refused. He said, "Why would I come such a long way and stand outside? Let me have the best part of this adventure. Let me also explore this cave". Draco said, "Okay then, but I am already telling you, you won't be able to see anything inside the cave". Drake said, "Doesn't care. At least I will be able to experience the creeps and chills within the cave". Draco said, "Okay then, let's go in". They both walked in there.

Draco saw the inscriptions on the walls; these inscriptions were of a small animal with three heads, and again, stick beasts throwing stones on it. Drake couldn't see anything as his sight was not so good. Draco kept walking further and saw the beast illuminati symbol and under it was written, "Mabel ivel struit Ascorn, Wofcorn ol Morcorn". Draco said to himself, "Wait a minute, what is this? Could it be that these are the names of Kampon's three brothers?" Drake asked, "What happened sire?" Draco said, "No nothing. Let's keep moving". They kept on moving forward. After sometime, Draco saw the portrait of the person in black robe, But now, there were some words written under that too, "Mabel ivel struit Ultimox Draco". Draco felt really suspicious now. They walked even further and saw the cauldron; this cauldron was of dark green color. This also had the inscriptions in dead languages. Draco breathe fire on this cauldron too. It was about to blast. Draco got hold of Drake's hand and ran out of the cave.

They both went back to the castle. At the castle, Draco said to Dorgard, "Dorgard. I have seen some strange things in the cave this time". Dorgard said, "What did you see your majesty?" Draco said, "First of all, I learned the name of Kampon's brothers, Ascorn, Wofcorn and Morcorn". Dorgard said, "Interesting, and what else?" Draco said, "And remember I told you about the person in black robe, under that it was written something like, Mabel ivel struit Ultimox Draco". Dorgard thought for some time and said, "I think I need to leave, now". Draco said, "Great. Finally you are leaving. Be fast. Come back as soon as you can". Dorgard said, "Yes your majesty". Dorgard's luggage was already packed, so he left.

CHAPTER 12
DAYS WITHOUT DORGARD

Dorgard had left, the castle felt really empty without him. Draco didn't have anything to do. Even if there would be any cases, it wouldn't be fun without Dorgard, without his sense of humour. Dorgard was the happiness of the court, his sense of humour, his respect towards everyone, the way he behaved, he was the highlight of the court. Everyone was really bored. There was no court jester. They didn't need a jester; Dorgard was the one who would entertain everyone.

It had been a week since Dorgard had left. Draco was on his throne with his palm on his face. The ministers were standing in their positions. The maids were getting the table ready for the breakfast. Drake was up in his room. Volinoir Draco was also in his room. Everyone was bored, nothing to do, nothing to entertain. That was how it would be every day. But this day, Volinoir Draco came downstairs a little earlier than usual. "Dad." Draco said, "Why are you down so early today?" Volinoir said, "Draco, my son. I have something to tell you, something important". Draco said, "Yes". Volinoir took a deep breath and said, "Okay, I can't keep this from you anymore. You're, you're, you're!!!" Draco said, "Yes, what am I?"

Volinoir took a deep breath and said, "You're..............." "The breakfast is ready", a maid interrupted.

They all went to the table and had their breakfast.

After the breakfast, Draco asked his father, "Dad, what am I?" Volinoir thought for some time and said, "No, nothing, forget I said something to you". Draco said, "I did". He went back and sat on his throne. Volinoir went to his room, shut the door tightly and burst out in tears. He was holding his tears with in all the time. He sat on his bed and started crying out, softly but with a lot of tears.

Draco was again bored, sitting bored, waiting eagerly for Dorgard to come back. He didn't care about anything, except for Dorgard to come really fast with his answers. Draco closed his eyes and imagined Dorgard's appearance. His blue scales, golden horns, and the wrinkles on his face which were older than Draco.

After sometime, Draco started thinking about what his father was trying to tell him. He thought for some time, and got the worst idea ever. He thought that he was adopted. But if that was the case, then how did he get the crown on his head? So thinking this would be useless. Draco stopped thinking of this and was eventually again lost, thinking about Dorgard, how he would be, where he was, did he find the answers or not.

After a few hours, they all had their lunch. Draco could see that his father's eyes were a little wet and his face looked sticky. Draco ignored it and continued eating.

After the lunch, he returned to his throne. He went back to his thinker mood, gone into a deep thought.

When the moon had taken place of the sun, everyone was called for dinner. After the dinner, everyone would go to their room and sleep.

That was their routine for their daily life after Dorgard was gone. No fun or fights, only waiting, for him to return, with answers

CHAPTER 13

DORGARD RETURNS

Days without Dorgard were very simple and boring, nothing good to do, just simply sit on the throne and wait.

One day, King Draco received a passenger phoenix coming in his castle. It had a letter, from Dorgard. Without thinking even once Draco took the letter from its feet and read the letter, it said:-

Your Majesty,

I am returning to beast lande by tomorrow morning. I have found someone who can answer all your questions. Be ready for my arrival.

Yours Sincerely, Dunhardol Dorgard

Draco felt really happy on knowing that his beloved detective is coming back with answers. He made arrangements for a welcome fiesta for Dorgard. They had made really great food for the party.

Dorgard had come the next morning very early. Draco saw Dorgard and a gentle smile spread on his face, he got up and walked towards him with his arms wide apart and said, "Dorgard! You have come back". He hugged Dorgard. Dorgard said, "I am sorry your majesty but I am a little late". Draco started looking around and said, "Where is the person who was going to answer my questions?" Dorgard said, "Your Majesty, he is a million years old beast, He is the one who created the 7 beasts. We need to go to him for the answers. But the problem is that he talks very formally and in a voice as old as sand. So it will be hard to understand him". Draco said, "Okay, we will leave next morning. Tonight we are having a feast for you".

They enjoyed a lot at the feast. They slept really late that night but had to wake up early.

They woke up next morning earlier than usual, they got ready to leave. They left at the time they used to wake up.

It was a really long trip, totally on foot. Dorgard was the one who was leading them. He led them through caves, mountains, forests and villages.

It was one o clock in the night; when they were in forest, they finally came close to their destination. "Look over there", Dorgard said pointing at a small hut in the woods, "that's the place where he lives".

They walked towards that hut. Dorgard knocked on the door. A voice came from inside, "Thou may comes in Dorgard". Everyone were puzzled about how did he know it was Dorgard. The door opened, everyone looked inside, they saw a really very old bald head humanoid beast. He had a beard which reached till his feet. He had blue skin and watery eyes of the same color. He didn't wear any clothes, he didn't need to. His beard covered his whole body. He was sitting on a chair in the middle of the room. There was no place for everyone to come in. Only Draco, Dorgard, Kampon and his brothers came in. Koonan had removed the roof and place Troopy and Croopy on his shoulders.

"Oh thy dear children", said the old man, "Thou hath grown a lot from the previous times hath thy seen thou". Draco whispered to Dorgard, "What is he talking?" Dorgard said, "You will understand soon". The old man continued, "Thou must have been forgotten thee. Thy be the creator of all of thou. Thy be Mosteraun Wolzakrus". Draco asked, "What is this, Mostorous wolfakrus?" Dorgard said, "It's his name, now please be quite so we may listen to him". The old man continued, "Lon Descretes Velinzer Ultimox Draco". Draco interrupted again, "How do you know my name?" This time Dorgard said, "Your majesty, for the sake of your crown, sit down and let him speak". Draco kept silent and sat. The old man continued. "Oh mighty King Draco, Thou hath a lot of doubts over thee. I give thine the permission to ask thee thou questions. Thy will give you the explanation".

CHAPTER 14

EXPLANATION

King Draco took his chance to clear all his doubts and asked, "Will thou…. Oh forget it. I can't speak that formally. Whatever, so listen to my first doubt, who were those beasts, who I have never met and they call me their enemy?" Mosteraun spoke, "Oh my child, Thou must not worry about them. Thou has already taken care of them. They were thy enemies, they were thy negative beasts, thou will understand all this, but not now, thy shalt explain it to thou". Draco was really confused about it. But he proceeded with his second doubt and asked, "Okay so, I had gone to destroy the cauldrons, but there I saw strange symbols and inscriptions. Will you explain that to me?" The old man spoke, "those, my child, those were revelations, written with blood on the walls of the cave. Those inscriptions narrated the stories of the creation of thy beasts, The words quoted beneath the beast illuminati symbol were, Mabel ivel struit, Which translates into, Will he kill, translated from beast Latin. Thy beast in black robe is thy negative beast. Thy will explain that later. The words written on the cauldron in Beast Latin narrated the creation of thy beasts". Draco said, "One more doubt, if you can understand normal language, why can't you speak normally?!" The old man laughed gently and said, "Thy normal tongue is what thy speak. Formal, is normal. Thou modern beasts has made strange new words and style, that is not normal". Draco said, "Wow, you explain really well. I will also try to speak formally, I mean normally. But not now, there is no time for that now". Suddenly, Koonan asked, "Listen here sire, if you are the one who has created us all, will you please prove it somehow?" The old beast sighed and spoke, "What kind of time is this? Thy has to give proof to my own children that thy has created them. But still, listen, thee knowest all of thy secrets". Koonan said, "Okay so, tell me, what my favorite food is?" The old beast said, "Young penguins". Koonan said, "That was easy, now tell, what is my favorite color?" The old beast said, "Blue". Koonan said, "Wow, either you are really smart, or you are my creator". Draco said, "If you are the person who has created all these 7 beasts, then tell how you created them". Monsteraun said, "Okay so listen. First thy shall narrate the creation of Koonan, the snow monster beast".

CHAPTER 15

CREATION OF KOONAN

The old man started to narrate the creation of Koonan. "It is for me to speak oh auspicious king and his beasts, First let thee say how thy got the ability to create life. When thy was 102 years old, thy father had left this unfair world, thee was a sorcerer. Thee gave me the ability to give life to the dead using cauldrons. But at one time, thy won't give life to 1 beast, but two different kinds, good and bad. There would be a positive beast and a negative beast. Now let thee narrate the story of Koonan. Thy speak it was approximate 990,000 years ago, Thy was 10,000 years old at that time. Thy be in Delewarete, Thy had seen with my own vision that a few beasts were throwing stones at an innocent big polar bear". "STOP!!!" Koonan shouted. Draco asked, "What happened?" Koonan said, "I don't, I suddenly got the feeling of being thrown stones at". Draco said, "forget it, let him continue". Monsteraun continued, "Thy had seen that, those tyrants threw stones at the innocent bear, until it fell down on the ground, it had been clear that was dead. Those tyrants walked away smiling and laughing, without even looking back at the sin they had made. Thy walked towards the deceased body of the innocent bear, Thy could see it, the tears flowing from its eyes. The creature was crying while he was being hit by stones, and it had been crying even after its death. Thine tears had struck tears in thy eyes. Thy put my hand on its forehead to understand why was he being hit? Thy found out that it was being hit for he was too large and unsuitable to live. Thy felt the living rage inside myself, thy wanted to bring it back to life, but thy was afraid of thee negative beast and its consequences. But thy had to make this decision. Thy decided to bring it back to life.

Thy took a blue cauldron and went into a nearby cave. There, thy cut the throat and took its blood and mixed it with potions in the cauldron and after all the magic, thy took the potion and poured it through the cut thy made in its throat. The cave smelled of blood and carcass, soon the smell increased. It was a sign that it is working.

The cut on its throat had been filled with skin, all the wounds and marks done by the stones were gone. But, the hair from his palms, feet, frontal torso and his face, fell off and his skin turned dark blue, his face became less projected like, its face became more flat and it got many wrinkles. Just then, thy remembered that to make it alive, thy had to mix another creature's blood with it. Thy had mixed the blood of a gorilla. So it started to look more like a gorilla. It woke up, and he was reborn. Thy namest him, Koonan. It had the strength of a hundred beasts put together. Thy noticed that even after thee beast was born, there were no negative beast. Thy felt joy within thy heart but just then, a dinosaur jumped out of the cauldron. It had to be the negative beast, which thy created. Thy namest it Undord.

Thy raised both of them, with equality. Thy taught Undord about being good but it would never listen, always up to some disobedience. It used to make practical jokes a lot, but slowly it turned out to be wicked. After it was 20 years old, it ran away from my house.

When Koonan was old enough to live by himself, a hundred years old, thy sent him back to Frostey Snowlande to live by himself. Thee hath now grown up and don't remember me, naughty child". Draco said, "So you mean, the dinosaur king was the negative beast of Koonan?" The old man said, "Yes. Thou are right". Draco said, "Wow, now I understood what those symbols inside the cave meant". Draco noticed something, Koonan was crying. Draco said, "Hey Koonan, what has happened?" Koonan said, "He is telling the truth. I remember all that happened to me". Draco said, "Come on, there is nothing to cry about in that, lets listen to him continue, with other stories of creation".

CHAPTER 16

CREATION OF TROOPY AND CROOPY

The old man spoke, "Listen thy children, thou shalt now listen to the tale of the creation of Troopy and Croopy, the tree beasts". "Wait a minute", Troopy interrupted, "Before I know how I was created, will you please tell me what my age is?" Monsteraun said, "Thy age be 900,000 years". Troopy said, "Wow, never realized that". Monsteraun said, "May thy begin telling thine tale?" Troopy said, "Yes of course, please continue". The old man begin, "It's for thy to speak, oh auspicious king and his beasts, that thy be the age of 100,000 at time, Thy was taking a walk during the dawn at the Derek Mohaun Forest. Thy had seen it, that there were many civilized beasts, cutting down trees. Thy could see it, thee trees were being cut down to the ground. The smell of the fresh leaves dying was, everywhere. Thy knew that, thee was doing it for thee own reason. But thy noticed that, there were two trees, normal, just like the every other tree. But those trees hadn't been cut; they were being thrown stones at. Thy would love to walk to those woodcutters and ask, "Oh woodcutters, why art thy throwing stones at these innocent trees?" But thy couldn't make up the guts. Thy stood there at my place, not moving, as if thy had been paralyzed.

Those woodcutters kept throwing stones at the innocent trees, until the leaves left the green color and turned brown, the bark became soft and weak, the trunk became weak as if it would fall with a blow of wind. Until, the tree would be dead. Yes, thy tree had been killed; those two innocent trees had been stoned, till death. Thy never understood these unfair laws of the nature. The innocent creatures who had made no sin in their whole life, they be killed, with a slow, and painful death. Those cruel creatures who have made nothing except for sins, they live a happy life.

Thy walked closer to the remains of the deceased trees. Thine trees could reach to heaven, but thy be the one who could stop it. Thy had the power, to bring thee back to earth, give thee a new life, another chance. But thy was again eaten by the fear of the negative beast. Thy had already created a negative beast, a trouble, which thy didn't know where was and what trouble was it creating. But thy always thought about the good thy was creating. Thy had been given this power for a reason, so thy must use it.

Thy uprooted the tree using thy telekinesis powers. Thy didn't find any cave nearby, so thee had to take them to beast lande to seek a cave. Thy found a cave inside a hill.

Thy took a brown cauldron. But there was a problem, trees doesn't have any blood. Thy had to do something about it but. Thy took a leaf which was still green, thy twisted it and from it, dropped some of the liquid of the trees, Thy doesn't knowest what it's called, but it gave the leaves its green colour. Thy mixed the blood of a monkey with it and after all the magic was done, thy makest a small cut in the trunk of both of those trees and poured the potion in both of them. Soon, the cut was filled, the trunk became tougher and broader, the leaves increased in number and were really dark green. Thee both got up on thine roots. Thy face got carved within the wood, and thou became, the living tree beasts, Thy had the power of sudden stealth, Thy namest them, Troopy and Croopy. Thy looked at the cauldron, expecting for the negative beast to come out, suddenly, a black unicorn, with red eyes jumped out. Thine darkness could make thee invisible at the night. Thine could be seen only by his red eyes, which were red as blood, Thy namest it Anchor. Thy treated all three of them equally. Thy taught Anchor about being good, but thee also had sworn never to be good. Anchor had run away from thy house after thee be 100 years old, thee had just left without telling to thy. Thy had left Troopy and Croopy in the Derek Mohaun Foreste after they were 200 years old. Thou hath forgotten me, after all this time, naughty children". Draco said, "Wow, art thou serious? I mean, are you serious?" The old man said, "from when thy mouth opens to time when thy concludes, Thy speakest only the truth". Draco said, "wow. Can't believe this". They saw that Troopy and Croopy were also crying. Draco said, "Wow, he is really telling the truth". Troopy cried, "all the memories suddenly popped up in front of my eyes". Draco said, "Okay, Don't worry. It's not a big deal". Croopy said, "you don't know how it feels". Draco said, "We will talk about that later. But first lets listen to more stories of creations".

CHAPTER 17
CREATION OF KAMPON

The old beast begun, "It is for thy to speak, oh auspicious king and his beasts, that once when thy be 120,000, thy had been on a walk in a forest of Beast lande, there, Troopy and Croopy were at home that time with anchor. Thy had been wandering in the forest, when thy came across something which gave me a déjà vu. Thy had seen a few civilized beasts throwing stones at a tree, again. But this time, I noticed that it was not the tree they were throwing stones, it was something on the tree. Thy wasn't able to see it. Slowly, the thing on the tree became visible to thy eyes. It was a green colour little chameleon which had again made no sin in his life. Those fiends hit it, but I couldn't stop them to do that. Thy walked closer to them and said them, "dear friends, it is not good to hurt an innocent creature". Then those wretched creatures started throwing stones at thy. Thy had no choice but to flee away from there.

Thy returned to that place after a half an hour, Thy expected those wretched ones to leave, and they had. Thy saw the small deceased body of the innocent chameleon, its eyes shut tight, and its mouth open with its tongue out and blood dripping down. Thy walked towards the deceased body of the innocent little life. Thy picked its body up, it looked so adorable, Why would anyone want to kill it? Thy decided to bring it back to life.

Thy brought its body to home. At home, Troopy, Croopy and Anchor, all of them asked thy, what is it? Why had I bought it? Thy didn't have the time to give them explanation, thy took a green cauldron and set out to seek another cave.

Thy found a big cave inside a forest, Thy put the cauldron at its end and started to create the potion.

It was difficult to create a potion for this chameleon, as his skin was really tough and his throat was really big. Thy took the blood of a wombat to mix with in the potion.

Thy put all the necessary things in the cauldron and stirred it. The cauldron started giving its colour. It was a sign, the potion was ready. Thy poured the potion into the throat of this creature.

Slowly it started to show signs of life, it got bigger in size, big as a wombat. And had another power, it could disappear into thin air. Thy named it, Kampon. Thy looked into the cauldron, waiting for the negative beast to come out.

An eagle flew out of the cauldron and started flying in the cave. Thy named it, Everet the eagle.

Thy took them both to my house, all of thy children would often have quarrels, but I would solve them soon.

As they grew up, Anchor and Everet became even more mischievous and trouble makers. But that slowly turned into wickedness and cruelty. As they grew up, they started to enjoy even more in troubling others. Not only troubling, soon they started irritating innocent people till they got angry. They took even more enjoyment in brutality and ruthlessness. And after getting old enough, they ran away from my house and started making menace around the planet. Thy had always taken great care of Kampon, but thou has also forgotten thee now, Naughty child". Now Kampon had burst out in tears. Everyone looked at him. Draco said, "Don't cry Kampon, we all are listening to our creations. We all have to go through this". Kampon said, "The way he is describing everything, everything is flashing before my eyes". Draco said, "I know it feels sad, but it's not compulsory to cry". Kampon said, "if it happened to you, you would burst into tears like a little baby!" Draco got angry on this and said in an angry pitch, "how dare you insult the king?" Kampon said, "stop behaving as if you are the greatest person on this planet and you can kill anyone who even talks in an angry tone to you". Koonan said, "Okay okay stop fighting you both". They made an eye contact for some time and then looked back at monsteraun. Draco said, "Okay so, will you please continue the tales".

CHAPTER 18
CREATION OF KAMPON'S BROTHERS

The old beast spoke, "It is for thy to speak, oh auspicious king and his beasts, that now thy is going to tell the tale of the creation of Ascorn, Wofcorn and Morcorn". Draco interrupted, "oh so those are their real names. I thought so. Okay, please continue". Monsteraun continued, "pay attention to what thy speakest. This is one of thine greatest story. Troopy, Croopy, Anchor and Everet had left thee. Kampon was thy only child still there. It had been difficult for thy to raise Kampon alone, thee had no friends to play with.

Thy went out on a walk, to seek some beast in trouble who thy could bring back to life. Thy again saw it, what thy sees for usual. Thy saw a group of villagers throwing stones at another innocent chameleon, Thy wasn't happy on seeing this, faith in love for everything, there was nothing related to that happening. Thy would ask them to stop, but thee knew that they would throw stones at thee. Thy hid behind a tree as they hit it even after it fainted. Thy noticed something strange, the chameleon had three heads, such a rare sighting, and they killing it? What a shame. Thy stood there and watched it all.

After they left, thy walked to the blood covered deceased body of the small chameleon with three heads, three brains, three souls, three lives. Three tongues lying out of their mouths with blood dripping from each of them. Thy took their deceased body to my home, thy didn't let kampon see it.

Thou takest a dark green cauldron and had left to seek another cave. Thy had found a big cave within the forest. Thy put the cauldron in it and started making the potion.

This one was confusing. Shall thy cut all the three throats or just one throat? Thy decided to cut all the three throats. Thy took the blood from all the three throats.

Thy mixed it with the blood of wombat too. Thy stirred the potion in the cauldron until it would be ready. It was ready soon. Thy poured it down all the three throats.

They started showing signs of life. But, the three heads started to form different bodies for themselves. And there were not three heads, but three chameleons. Three different living breathing bodies. All of those three got bigger like Kampon did. They had the same power as Kampon but there was a problem. They couldn't talk. They didn't have any vocal cords. Thy named them, Ascorn, Wofcorn and Morcorn. Thy looked at the cauldron, waiting for the negative beast to pop out.

Suddenly, a skeleton of a saber toothed tiger jumped out. It was the size of a normal saber toothed tiger. Thy was afraid what would it do after it grew up. Thy named him, Secroop.

Thy took all four of them home. Thy introduced all of them to Kampon. Thy said to Kampon that these 3 art thy brothers. Keep good care of them. As time passed, Secroop's size and madness increased. At the age of hundred, thee be the size of a small hill. Thee ran away from my house and begin his madness elsewhere. After they were old enough, Kampon and his brothers left thine house. They are also old now, and have forgotten me, naughty children". They three also started crying. Draco said, "Thank you sir. You have given us all the answers. We must be leaving now". Monsteraun said, "Stop, doesn't thou wants to listen to the story of the creation of the 8th beast?" Everyone got puzzled on this. Draco said, "What do you mean? Who is this 8th beast?" Monsteraun answered in a calm voice, "Who could it be? Its thou. King Lon Descretes Velinizer Ultimox Draco. Oh sorry, Thy meant, Lord Ultimox Draco".

CHAPTER 19

THE CREATION OF
THE EIGHTH BEAST

Draco said, "What do you mean by Lord Draco? What do you mean by I am the eighth beast? There are only 7 beasts". Monsteraun said, "No, my child, this is the most interesting tale thy is going to tell thou". Draco said, "No! No more tales, I just want explanation". Mosnteraun said, "Thou won't be able to understand without knowing the full tale". Draco said, "Alright, fine, continue". The old beast spoke, "It hath been said by me to you, oh auspicious king and his beasts, that once when thy had been the age of 120,000, thy had been tired of creating life. Thy had decided to bring back one last beast to life, but this time, it won't be any normal beast I find, it shall be a really powerful and helpful beast. Draco, Thou hath been named after Lord Ultimox Draco right?" Draco nodded. Monsteraun said, "What if thy says that thou hasn't been named after Lord Ultimox Draco, The Messenger of Sedcas. But, thou is, Lord Ultimox Draco". Everyone was startled. Draco exclaimed, "What do you mean, old beast?" Monsteraun said, "Thou must have forgotten. But thou is Lord Ultimox Draco". Draco said, "NO!! I am the son of King Volinoir Draco. And how did I get this crown on my head if I am the Lord?" Monsteraun said, "Thou will know, first you must listen to the tale of thy creation". Draco said, "Okay then, continue".

Monsteraun begun, "Oh thy lord, Pay attention to what thy speakest. When thy was 120,000 years old, thy time had finished. Lord Ultimox Draco had come to thee, to collect thy soul.

Thy noted that there were bruises on thou face. Quoth thy, "Oh thy Lord, what hath happened that thy must see these bruises on thine face". Thou spokest, "It hath been done by the evil devil. Thee hath done that to me in the battle of gods against devils, a billion years ago". Thy quoted again, "Thou mean that these bruises were done a billion years back". Thou spoke, "Yes. Thou art right". Thee said, "Why doesn't it fades away?" Thou said, "This hath been done by the leader of the devils, the beast Satan. Thy hath slain him 25 million years after thee had put this marks on my face, but it was his curse that these bruises shall always disturb thee, throughout thy life". Thy asked, "Wait, does thou means Satan is dead?" Thou spokest, "Yes, but the evil being created these days hath been done by Satan's devil companions. They are trying their best to revive Satan". Thy said, "Oh no, what if thy succeeds in reviving that Devil?" Thou was about to speak. Suddenly, we were under attack. Those Devils attacked over us. Thy had been afraid and retreated within thy house. Thou were fighting outside against those devils.

After half an hour, thy left my house and walked outside. Thy had seen it, thine deceased body. Those devils had taken thy life. Blood oozed from thy blessed body, from the cuts and bruises, thy was really brave, and still art. God had the power to revive thou, but thee doesn't does everything automatically. I had to take part in that. Thy hath decided to revive thou.

This time, thy had taken the blood of a Dragon, an ancestor of the Draco Dynasty. Thy had taken it to a cave, which even thy doesn't remember where is it. This time, thy had taken a dangerous cauldron. It was dark black, and whenever thee goes close to it, thee gets a headache. It was the only cauldron, powerful enough which could revive a lord.

Thy sliced thee throat and took the blood from it. Thy mixed the blood of the dragon and mixed all the things in the cauldron and stirred it. Even while stirring, thy was falling unconscious by the cauldron but thy had to be awake. After the potion was ready, thy poured it on thine throat.

Thou got up; thine bruises disappeared from thine face and body. Thou had got a crown of flesh on thy head. Thou had been reborn, as Lord Ultimox Draco. Thy watched the cauldron waiting for the negative beast to come. This negative beast was the most dangerous thing thy hath ever created. A humanoid beast wearing a black robe, thy face was completely covered, by darkness. Thy face couldn't be seen by the shadow of the hood. Thee was the most evil thing one could imagine. Thy called himself The Son of Satan. Thy name him, Dark Shadow.

One day, thy left Draco and Dark Shadow at home and went out for a walk. On thy return, thy had seen that there were two red spots on the fore head of Shadow. Those spots were red as blood, and shined really bright. Thy assumed it to be his eyes which had opened recently.

Dark Shadow became really evil. Soon it left the house and joined all the negative beasts and did huge attacks and fights with Draco. Thy is really very bad".

Draco exclaimed, "Oh!! So that's why they were calling me their enemy. But how did I forget all this? And how was I reborn as a child at my father's place?" Monsteraun continued, "As they were continuously attacking on thou, thy made you be born again, as the son of Lon Descretes Evenisor Volinoir Draco. Thy had given thou a new identity. Thou were reborn, as Lon Descretes Velinizer Ultimox Draco. Thou had no memory of thine past life". Draco said, "Interesting. Tell me more about Shadow".

CHAPTER 20

DARK SHADOW

Monsteraun spoke, "There is not much to speak about him. The only thing no one can ignore is that thee is the most evil beast on the planet. Thee is a devil. Let thy tell thou more about it. Thee is thine negative beast.

No one knows where thee is right now. But where ever must thee be, thy menace and violence must be going on. Draco and Shadow would fight really often. Thee eyes were bright red, but thy doesn't knows why didn't thine eyes showed up on thee creation. Must be that thee species was the kind of that.

Thee would sometimes abuse thy also. No respect for the creator, what a shame. Thy doesn't understand why, but it had run away from me earlier than all the other negative beasts, it had run away when it was only 36 years old. After both of thee had left thy, Thy quest was complete. Thy had completed the 8 beasts. For someone's reference, thy had made markings in the cave, which said about thou origins and left a Satan symbol which meant what if Satan would kill my beast. And also thy drew a portrait of Dark Shadow, and had written the stories of beast creations on the cauldron in Beast Latin.

Thy emptied my home and retreated into this forest. This hut was big enough for thy to live, only thy. Thy hasn't eaten anything from the past 800,000 years. Thy doesn't needs to.

One day, Dark shadow had attacked on thy. He had asked me to give thy the Dark Cauldron. Thy doesn't knowest the reason thee was making the strange command, but thy didn't tell me.

Thee tortured me a lot but thee didn't speak. Thee tortured me until thy fell unconscious.

When thy woke up, Dark Shadow wasn't visible there. Thee was gone, but till today it troubles thy about why did the devil want the cauldron". Draco said, "very well, now will you please tell me about the Dark Cauldron?"

Monsteraun said, "Wish thy could, but thy hath nothing to say about it". Draco said, "at least you know about it more than I do. Tell me everything you know".

CHAPTER 21

THE DARK CAULDRON

Monsteraun spoke, "Oh my Lord, my king thine argument is undefeatable. Thou always finds a way to outwit thy. Now thy hast got no choice except for talking about the dark cauldron". Draco said, "Okay, thank you. Now let's begin talking about the cauldron". Monsteraun said, "Yes, So here is what thy knowest about the cauldron. The cauldron is called, the dark cauldron. It is named that as it is in the darkest shade of black. It is so dark, that the darkness of cave of nogletune would look bright when compared to it". Draco said, "Hey wait a minute. Have you ever been to that cave? Pretty dark right?" Monsteraun said, "yes it is. Now let thy continue". Draco said, "yes please, continue".

Monsteraun continued, "So, as thy had been telling, it has something coming from it which gives us a headache. Thy doesn't knowest what it is called, but it gives a really strong feeling in the head. It's really dangerous. So, if thou stands close to it for an hour or 2, than", Draco interrupted, "Will we die?" Monsteraun continued, "yes we will die". Draco said, "so it's a dangerous too". Monsteraun said, "it's the most dangerous thing. It has created the most evil beast of all time". Draco questioned, "me?"

Monsteraun answered, "no not you, I was talking about Dark Shadow".
Draco said, "oh okay". Monsteraun said, "seriously sir, Thou is the lord.
But thou hath taken foolishness to the next stage". Draco asked, "what
did you say?" Monsteraun said, "no nothing". Everyone started giggling.
Monsteraun said, "Okay so let thy continue. And the dark cauldron is
really rare. Because that is the only way, Dark shadow can be killed, but
there is a problem. If thou destroy a cauldron, only the negative beast
would be deceased. But if thou destroy the dark cauldron, then all the
8 beasts and Dark Shadow, all of them will be destroyed, and also, thy
will be too. Most likely, thy hath to die". Draco said, "I don't understand".
Monsteraun said, "Let thy explain thou. This Dark Cauldron holds the
power of all the beasts, if it's destroyed, then we all shall die". Draco
asked, "wait, but why would you die?" Monsteraun said, "does thou
knows how am thy living such a long life? Thy life expectancy was only
around 100,000 years. But thy enlarged it because of that cauldron, it
holds thy power too". Draco said, "It's so interesting".

Suddenly, the clock struck 12:00. Draco said, "Oh, I need to go. I am
sorry". Monsteraun said, "no thou art not going anyway". Draco said, "I
am sorry, I need to go, its really late". Monsteraun said, "no. thou are
going to slay Dark Shadow". Draco said, "have you gone crazy at this
second?" Monsteraun said, "no, thy prophecy had said that the person
who I would be talking at twelve will be the one to slay Dark Shadow".

CHAPTER 22
RETURN TO BEAST LANDE

Everyone was startled on listening that, "what do you mean? what prophecy?" Monsteraun said, "when thy had been worried about where Shadow is and what mess is thee creating. Thy prayed to god for some solution. That night, thy had a dream. It showed thy talking to another beast, about slaying Dark Shadow. The main thing I remember is that the clock struck 12 at night. So I took it as a prophetic dream telling me that the person who is going to slay Dark Shadow will be talking with me at twelve". Draco said, "Wow, pretty much a co incidence". Monsteraun said, "It isn't a co incidence. It's a prophecy. If thou wouldn't stay here, then thy must come with you, to thy castle". Draco didn't know what to answer to that. He was confused. He answered after a pause, "Okay you can come with use, but I don't think an old person like you can walk that long distance". He laughed a bit and answered, "oh Lord, how can thy speak such non sense. Thy may be old, but thy is healthy as a young and gallant man". Draco said, "okay then. come with us". They set their right foot and begun their journey back home, to Beast Lande.

The way back was really tough. It was not a good decision to begin a journey during the night. It was dark, but they all had good eye sight as they had been through that cave. But still the darkness of night is a different thing.

They passed through mountains and valleys and forests and lakes and many more places. The way back seemed way longer than the way to go. The next morning, they had reached a lot much closer to beast lande. After a lot of time, they reached within the boundaries of their kingdom.

After a really long journey, they reached back to beast lande. All the citizens were happy to see them return. They walked to the castle.

When they reached to the castle, Draco's father was happy to see them, but on seeing Monsteraun, he was startled and he said, "You?" Monsteraun smiled and said, "Yes, it is thy, Oh mighty king". He asked, "Why are you here?" Monsteraun answered, "Thine son, Thy mean the lord, is going to slay Dark Shadow". Volinoir asked, "What? Why? Explain clearly". Monsteraun said, "It is not for thy to explain, but for thou to understand. Thy had seen in a prophecy that Draco is going to slay Shadow". Volinoir said, "No! I can't let this happen. What if he dies?" Monsteraun said, "Thee hath to die. That is the only way shadow can die". Draco interrupted, "Wait a minute, you never told that I am going to die". Monsteraun said, "Son, thy hath told thou. The only way to finish

Dark Shadow, is by destroying the Dark Cauldron. But after that, thee all have to die". Draco said, "Isn't there any other way?" Monsteraun said, "This be the only option". Draco said, "Oh god, it means I have to die?" Monsteraun said, "If thou want to slay Shadow". Draco said, "Then forget it, I won't slay him, I won't die. And he hasn't done anything bad right". Monsteraun said, "Thy cannot be sure. But thy can be sure that thee will soon return and wreck havoc". Draco said, "At least hope he doesn't come to Beast lande".

Suddenly, they heard a bang outside, and citizens crying and shouting for help. Draco said, "No, please tell me that I am dreaming". Koonan said, "I am sorry sire, but this is real". Draco said, "Dorgard, find out what is happening outside". Dorgard went up to the balcony and looked outside. While he was up, everyone started thinking what would happen and whispered among themselves.

Suddenly they heard Dorgard shout, "YOUR MAJESTY!! PLEASE COME UP!!! YOU NEED TO SEE THIS!!!!!" Everyone ran upstairs. They looked out from the balcony and saw, the sun wasn't visible even during the morning, dark clouds had covered the sky and there was a dark figure abusing citizens. It was Shadow, Dark Shadow, he has come. Draco said, "Speak of the devil and the devil appears". They heard Monsteraun's voice from behind, "Draco, Thou must go and protect thy people". They looked back and saw Monsteraun. He said, "Thou must go and help them, but first let thy give thou some advices. Some say, it is impossible to defeat Shadow at night, but this darkness is no lesser than night, so be careful.

And also, thou cannot kill him now. But at least you can scare him away, but destroying the planet is easier than scaring him away. Thou hath to work really hard for that, and also, the most important thing,

Never give up; Dark Shadow doesn't kill his enemies. Thee just disable them to the extent that thou must give up. But thou must not give up; death is more preferable than giving up. Wish you luck, oh lord".

Draco said, "It's dangerous". Monsteraun said, "So now, bravery has left thou, and thou have braced logic in its place. No problem let thine citizens die, then thou will be known as the most coward king ever". Everyone looked at Draco. Draco lowered his sight to the ground. He thought for some time and then looked up. He turned to face the city, and he jumped out and flew into the city to save it.

CHAPTER 23

CONFRONTING THE SHADOW

Draco glided into the city. He landed straight in front of shadow, but 10 meters away. Shadow said, "So, the lord returns. Giving pain to your innocent people is very interesting, Draco". Draco looked at shadow, they both made eye contact, "I remember you", Draco said, "I remember everything. My mind may have forgotten your appearance, but my eyes haven't I still remember you, from the day you were created, and I will remember you even after you die". Shadow laughed and said, "Oh my dear, Brother! Don't you know? When I die, you also must have to die. Oh of course you know, you are the one who should slay me, according to some stupid, meaningless and imaginary, Prophecy!" Draco was shocked on listening that he already knows about the prophecy. He question, "how," shadow interrupted, "How do I know huh? Come on Draco, Has logic left you, and in place of that, have you braced bravery?" Draco said, "Just a few seconds ago, Monsteraun had told me the exact opposite of this. Anyway, this doesn't answer my question". Shadow said, "That's what I mean, logic has left you. If you would use at least a little logic, then you would understand that I am a devil, and I can read minds. After the day I had tortured Monsteraun, that day I had read his mind that he himself doesn't knows where the cauldron is. I would kill him, because he was no use to me. But I let him live, just to see if that old thing would come to me for some use. I secretly spied on him to see what he would be doing. I saw him praying about some help to kill me. That night, I watched him as he dreamed. He dreamed about slaying me, talking to someone on that topic, the clock struck 12 that time. And didn't you notice me? The day you were talking, I was hidden in the shadow of the chair Monsteraun was sitting on, when the clock struck 12; I understood that it was only you, the one who would be dreaming about slaying me. So I attacked on your city. All this happened only because I let that old man live. That was the biggest great job I had done in my life". Draco said, "No, that was your biggest mistake". He said as he slapped Shadow on the face with his tail. The attack was so strong that dark shadow fell on the ground.

Dark shadow groaned as he fell on the ground. Draco said, "You let him live, because of that, I got to know about you, your weaknesses and how to slay you". Shadow got up angrily and cried, "You have done nothing good damned creature, it was your biggest mistake that you hit me!" He said as he pointed up to the sky, a lightning bolt fell down straight at Draco but he was fast enough to dodge it. His heart hammered to his ribs as he had experienced a near death experience. Shadow again pointed his hand at the sky this time the lightning bolt was faster and it hit straight in the head of Draco.

Draco fell down to the ground, as he saw everything fade away. He heard some voice, a voice familiar but unrecognizable. "Is that all?" The voice said, "The bravery, the wisdom, the power, the kindness, the boldness, is it all done? Was that all, your guts, your glory? Where is it? Is everything gone, if it is, then forget about your people, your life, your hard work, your success, and leave this world, and come to me. But if there is still some bravery left in that heart or the thing trapped within your ribs, then get up, get up and fight. Show the devil that you are still a Lord. Get up, go my child. Get up". Everything was fading away, but Draco managed to concentrate and get up. He got up on his legs, but he was still unconscious. Shadow said, "Oh so the Lord has lost all his power but is still trying to get up. Okay get up, you will soon give up". Draco walked a few steps, like a toddler learning to walk, but fell down on his knees after a few steps. Shadow walked close to him and laughed and said, "Give up now, you are nothing in front of a devil like me". Shadow was standing right in front of Draco. Draco looked up at Shadow's face.

He spit huge fireballs on his face. Shadow cried out loudly, "AAAHHHH!!! STOP IT!!! GO TO HELL!!!!" He started running here and there. Draco kept blowing fire on him until he didn't run away. Shadow was forced to flee away from there.

After Shadow had gone away from there, the weather was back to normal. Draco returned inside his castle.

That night, Monsteraun was very afraid of what was happening. He made his prayers and went to sleep. That night, he had another prophetic dream. He had seen the moon, straight above a mountain, and Satan standing on the mountain.

The next morning he said it to Draco, "Oh Lord, Last night thy had seen a strange dream. In thy dream, the full moon was straight above a hill, and thy had also seen Satan sitting atop of it". Draco said, "You don't need to worry, I will take care of it".

CHAPTER 24

FINAL FIGHT

The royal breakfast had been going on. Draco had already decided what to do with the prophetic dream Monsteraun had seen. He knew that Dark Shadow had seen the dream. He also knew that Dark Shadow, as a devil would love to find his leader, Satan. Dark Shadow would also come to the mountain. Draco just had to go to the mountain on the next full moon night when the moon would be straight above a mountain. The question arising was, which mountain would it be?

After the breakfast, Draco went to his throne. He was sitting on the throne, thinking about it. He looked at Dorgard, he knew Dorgard had answers to all the questions, but he chose to keep Dorgard away from this. After a lot of time, Draco had decided that, during the night, whichever mountain the full moon will be over the night, that mountain will be it.

The night time was about to come, the moon was still not visible. It was late evening time. The maids were cleaning the rooms. Draco was on his throne. Waiting for the moon to come out, for it will be easy for him to decide.

The night had come, the moon had risen. Draco went up to his room and out in the balcony, he looked at the moon, it was crescent. The moon wasn't full. Draco slept peacefully that night knowing that Dark Shadow was still spying on them. He acted as if he didn't know. Even Dark Shadow knew that Draco knew he was spying on them. But sadly, Draco didn't know that Dark Shadow knew that.

Dark Shadow slowly crept in to the room, without making a noise, he went into the mirror.

The next morning, Draco got up and went to Monsteraun. Monsteraun would always sleep on a chair, not a bed. He was used to the chair and a bed would be uncomfortable for him.

Draco walked into his room. He saw Monsteraun sitting on his chair with his eyes open. Draco said, "Monsteraun, did you see any prophetic dreams tonight?" Monsteraun said, "no, my lord". Draco went away from his room and went down to his throne.

He sat on his throne waiting for his ministers to assemble into their position. When they assembled, Draco got up and announced, "ministers, today we may get a bad news. If you get it, then don't panic, just report it to me". Everyone nodded.

They went for the breakfast, at the breakfast table; Draco was again in the deep thought about the dream and Dark Shadow.

Meanwhile, in Draco's room, Dark shadow was hidden in the mirror. He suddenly came out. He started walking around his room like a restless soul. He was actually looking for something.

Suddenly, he sensed someone coming; he went back into the mirror. He saw a maid in the room, she was cleaning the bed.

Draco was sitting on his throne, just then, he heard a maid shouting, "Your majesty, one of the maid has disappeared!!" Draco said, "Oh no! Don't worry, I will do something". Draco went to his room, he saw everything scattered and the room was a mess. Draco looked around for some clues. He saw some blood on the ground, he smelled it and said, "oh no, my sister has been kidnapped by that wretched devil".

He ran downstairs and announced it, "ONE OF THE MAIDS HAS BEEN KIDNAPPED BY DARK SHADOW!!!!" Everyone was disturbed by that, but the ministers didn't panic as they were ordered. Draco knew that Dark Shadow was going to do something. Dorgard came to Draco and said, "your Majesty, I am sorry for the loss so, will you let me investigate". Draco said, "no Dorgard, It's my fight, let me fight it by myself". Dorgard said, "now, you are acting like a real man. That's the spirit". Draco said, "thank you". Dorgard said, "wait, aren't you angry on me?" Draco said, "angry for what?" Dorgard said, "because, I was a little impolite". Draco smiled and said, "Dorgard. I have understood, I am a king, I am a Lord, but that doesn't mean I deserve all the respect on this planet". Everyone who heard that became emotional. A little tear flowed down Dorgard's eye. Draco said, "What? You are crying? Come on now. You are not acting like a real man now". Dorgard said, "your majesty, I, I am not able to describe the joy I am feeling on listening to you. You have finally realized what a true king is". Draco said, "yes, I have. A true king is not someone who gets all the respect, but the one who gives others the same amount of respect". Everyone burst out into tears. Draco said, "What? Everyone is crying? Come on now. If there is a reason to cry, it's because a maid has gone missing". Everyone changed their reason of crying. Draco said, "Okay everyone, Stop crying, I promise, I will get her back by tomorrow". Everyone's burden of worries got lesser.

That night, Draco looked out of his balcony; it was a full moon night. Draco took the chance and without telling anyone, He flew away from his balcony.

He followed the moon until he was directly below it, He was above a hill, he settled down and stood on the top of the hill. He looked around searching for him. He heard a mysterious laugh, it was the laugh of Dark Shadow, He looked behind and saw him. Draco said, "so you are here?

Tell me, where is Satan?" Draco said, "can't you see, he is right in front of you".

Draco was startled on listening to him and said, "You, No. You can't be Satan. He has got only one eye". Dark Shadow said, "so have I". Saying that, he took off his hood and for the first time, his face could be seen.

The two red spots, were not his eyes, they were wounds on his forehead. He had one eye above his nose. His eye, nose and mouth were in a complete straight line. He had two fangs coming out of his mouth.

Draco said, "NO!! Oh my god, this is not true! You, now I remember, those two wounds, I had scratched them on your fore head during a fight when we were young". Dark Shadow said, "Yes, finally you remember it. Okay then, the time has come for me, to take revenge from you, by scratching off your head". Draco said, "At my castle, people are worried; tell me where is the maid you have kidnapped!" Shadow said, "I have tied her, she is right behind me. If you want her back then fight me!" Draco looked behind him. He saw a female dragon tied to a tree, it was his sister. Draco said, "yes, I am ready. Let's fight". Dark Shadow said, "finally, you are behaving like a man".

They began fighting. Dark Shadow pointed his finger in the sky and a Lightning Bolt dropped down, But Draco dodged it. Draco spitted a fire ball on him, but he dodged it. Draco flew up in the sky and suddenly

came down and thwacked him with his tail. Dark Shadow fell down.
Draco said "A billion years ago, thy had slain thou. Now thy will again
slay thou, the second time". Saying this, Draco threw him down from the
hill. Dark Shadow left out a scream as he fell down from a great height
of a thousand meters.

Draco untied the maid from the tree and took her back to the castle. At
the castle, everyone was happy to see him and the maid. Monsteraun
asked, "Oh Lord, where had thy gone?" Draco said, "To fight with Dark
Shadow. Thy had discovered it that, Dark shadow was Satan". Monsteraun
said, "Wait, what thou mean by was?" Draco said, "Dark Shadow is dead,
Thy hath slain thee". Monsteraun said, "No. Thee cannot die. Thee will
be alive until the cauldron isn't destroyed. Even if thee hath died, thee
will return. Thee will be revived within a few days".

CHAPTER 25
THE FINAL FANTASY

Draco said, "What! Oh no?" Monsteraun said, "O lord, what will thy do now?" Draco said, "there is only one way, Thy must destroy the cauldron". Monsteraun said, "but, thy can't do that. Thou will also have to die". Draco said, "A small sacrifice to save a million others. It's nothing bad". Monsteraun said, "but thou is the lord". Draco said, "and thee be the Satan, so let's end the evil". Monsteraun sighed and spoke, "will miss you O lord. Thou is immortal. Thou will always live in our hearts. But thy also hath to die, So thy both will be together". Draco said, "Thou doesn't hast to worry about it. I will leave by tomorrow".

The next morning, Draco woke up as usual. He walked downstairs, but instead of sitting on the throne, Draco sat on the ground right in front of the throne. Dorgard came to him and said, "Your majesty, Why are you sitting on the floor?" Draco said, "I am worth for that, not to sit on a golden throne. Sell this throne and donate all the money for the poor and needy". Everyone was startled on listening to that. Dorgard said, "Your majesty, why have you become so pious?" Draco said, "because today is my last day on this planet". Everyone were even more startled. Dorgard asked in a stammering voice, "w-why your Majesty?" Draco said, "to slay the evil, thy must leave this planet". Dorgard tried to be calm and asked, "Your majesty but, When a Satan dies, the Lord also dies". Draco said, "at least there will be no evil". Dorgard said, "But there will be no good too". Draco said, "So it seems". Dorgard said, "So it is". Draco said, "But thy must slay him. Its my last day, so let me do something good for this planet. Sell all of our gold, sell all the precious things, spend our entire royal treasury, and give that to the poor. I don't want to die as a person who never helped the world". Everyone again started crying. Dorgard cried, "Your Majesty, we will do anything, please don't leave us". Koonan said, "Your majesty, I will keep a fast for a month but please don't die". Kampon said, "I promise I will always be polite with you, please don't leave". Draco laughed and said, "Oh my dear children, I don't need to be alive to be with you. I will always be with you. In your heart, in your happy times, celebrating with you, in your sad times, crying with you. But my dear 7 beasts, I am sorry to say that but you all must come with me". Koonan said, "Wait what?" Draco said, "Yes, if I die, you all will also die". Koonan said, "What do you mean? I am not going to die and I won't let you die". Draco said, "I am sorry. What has decided has been decided". They had no choice but to agree with him.

That day, Draco and the 7 beasts went to Monsteraun's room. Monsteraun was sitting on his chair. Draco and his beasts were surrounding him,

Draco said, "Monsteraun, Thy time has come to leave, so speak it up. Tell thy, how to destroy the cauldron". Monsteraun said, "Oh Lord, Destroying the Dark Cauldron is very painful. When thou gets close to it, thou gets a headache. To destroy it, first put thy head in the cauldron, and thy head will melt and then thou will be headless, next thy must blow fire on it with thy throat, and finally, fall to the ground, as thou dies, and the cauldron is destroyed". Draco said, "Its not difficult". Suddenly, they heard a scream, "Your Majesty, We are under attack!!!" Draco ran to the balcony and saw many soldiers in black armor. Draco asked, "Who are they?" Monsteraun's voice came, "They must be the dark devil soldiers". Draco said, "Oh no, Now what shall thy do?" Monsteraun said, "If thou destroy the cauldron, they all shall be deceased". Draco said, "Then what are we waiting for lets destroy the cauldron". Monsteraun said, "Thy doesn't knowest where the cauldron is". Draco said, "But thy knowest". Monsteraun said, "What? How?" Draco said, "When thy had thrown Shadow from the hill, thy had found a map, it showed the position of the cauldron, it's in a forest in the meeting point of Lon capturite and Beast Lande". Monsteraun said, "Then be fast, my lord, thou will be remembered".

Draco greeted his father, for the last time. Volinoir said, "Do you have to go son?" Draco said, "I never do anything without a reason". They hugged each other, for the last time.

Draco had left Monsteraun as a sign. If Monsteraun dies, it means his quest is complete.

Draco left. He went into the forest, the 7 beasts, Drake and the soldiers were fighting against the Devils. Draco was out on his quest. It was thunder storming out of his kingdom, he was fighting against the storm, it was the devils who were trying to stop him. They were trying to slow him until Dark Shadow revives. But Draco didn't give up; he continued to move on, through the storms.

Meanwhile, in his kingdom, the attack was getting stronger, but they didn't give up too. The 7 beasts were wearing their own armor. Drake had his armor and sword and shield. Sometimes, they would take a break and go in protection inside the castle. The substitute soldiers would be sent in their place. Monsteraun's chair was in the middle of the court room. Volinoir Draco, Dorgard, and the ministers and maids were surrounding him. Waiting for the call, the end of the quest. Monsteraun said, "His quest will soon be completed". Volinoir left the place and went behind a pillar. Dorgard followed him and saw, He was crying, the previous king, the father of the lord, he was crying. Dorgard said, "Your majesty, why are you crying?" He cried, "I knew that! I knew all that already! All this could be avoided, if I told him that already, he didn't have to go to that old beast and he wouldn't have to slay Dark Shadow, It's totally my fault!" Dorgard said, "You don't have to worry, he is sacrificing his life for something good". Volinoir said, "No, It was not his fault that Satan was born, so he doesn't needs to die to kill him". Dorgard said, "Yes he doesn't, but he is benefiting a million people even in his death. Please stop crying and come with us".

Volinoir went back and surrounded Monsteraun. He was still sad and depressed. His only son, not even his own son, was dying for the death of Satan. He knew it was good, but he couldn't even see his son's last face.

Draco was fighting his best through the storm; he was halfway through, when he suddenly fell to the ground exhausted. He decided to take a short break and rest there.

Meanwhile, the 7 beasts were fighting against those soldiers. After a lot of time, they walked into the castle. Koonan said, "it's enough everyone. We need to go to Draco! I wonder what his condition is". Dorgard said, "if you people want to go, then leave, and make sure he reaches to the cave alive". Koonan said, "alright, Come on beasts we've got some work to do". Volinoir said, "Stop!" They all looked at him, He said, "I won't come with you people but, make sure Draco is good". Koonan said, "With you as his father who has raised him, he will always be good". Volinoir smile and said, "Leave". Koonan said, "We will miss you all, remember us". Saying this, they left that place.

Dorgard said to Volinoir, "You, are really good sir". Volinoir said, "I know". They looked at monsteraun, waiting for him to die, so they may be assured that his quest is complete.

The 7 beasts ambushed through the soldiers and went away, into the storm. They traced the footprints of Draco and walked into the storm. After a lot of time, they saw Draco resting on the ground; they chose not to reveal themselves and hid behind rocks. After sometime Draco got up and continued his quest. He kept walking and walking. After a lot of time, he reached to the meeting point of Beast Lande and Lon Capturite. Now he had to search for the cave and more than half of the problem was finished.

"His quest will be completed soon", Monsteraun said sitting on his chair. All the people surrounding him were being worried even more. Dorgard said, "I need to admit it, King Ultimox Draco was the best king ever born in this dynasty". Volinoir said, "not in this dynasty, on this planet".

Draco had found the cave, he walked inside it. The seven beasts followed him silently. This cave had the biggest opening in all the caves. So big that even Koonan could fit in. Draco looked at the first inscription; it was of a dragon lord fighting with beasts outside a small house. Draco walked further. The beasts saw the first inscription. Koonan whispered, "this is exactly how Draco was fighting, I think". They followed Draco,

Draco saw the second inscription of beast illuminati and under that was written, "Mabel ivel struit inse mons Lord Ultimox Draco". Draco let down a few tears on reading that. He kept walking further. The 7 beasts went and looked at that inscription. Koonan whispered, "why would he cry on reading this". Draco saw the third inscription, "It was of Dark shadow and under that was written, "Welle, Karkondo threne donne thymon". On reading this, Draco burst out into tears. He continued to walk. The 7 beasts read it and said, "Why does he cry like a baby for this?" They continued to walk further.

"He is very close now", Monsteraun said. Everyone was even more worried. Volinoir said, "there are many brave soldiers outside, fighting bravely. To protect the castle a little more time and this pain will end". The soldiers and Drake, they all were fighting really hard.

Draco finally reached to the cauldron. His head ached by the cauldron, because it was very much radioactive. He stood on the other side of the cauldron. The cauldron didn't give out any light, it gave out direct fire.

Monsteraun said, "his quest is nearly completed". Just then, Drake walked in and said, "is it over?" Dorgard silenced him.

Koonan said, "Are you sure you want to do this?" Draco said, "I know it. That I am sure". Koonan said, "think again, this is your last chance. After this there is no turning behind". Draco sighed.

Monsteraun said, "he has almost done this". Drake also joined the people who were surrounding him. The soldiers were fighting bravely.

Draco said, "if we die doing good, we may get a chance of going to heaven". Koonan said, "but if we live, we can make heaven on the planet". Draco said, "maybe a heaven can be made on the planet, but the people who actually deserve it won't get the chance to enjoy it".

Monsteraun said, "Soon, his quest will be completed". Everyone was even more worried now.

Koonan said, "But atleast tell us why did you cry on reading that?" Draco said, "as always, it was written will he kill not the great Lord Ultimox Draco. And the final inscription said, Well, You have come, so you will be killed". Koonan said, "this will be the last decision you will make in your life, so choose wisely". Draco said, "that decision has already been made. But there is one more decision". Koonan asked, "What is it".

Monsteraun said, "it's nearly done, the worries will be finished". Everyone reached to the intense point of worries.

Draco answered, "the decision of going to heaven or hell". Saying this, he dipped his head in the cauldron, his head melted with the heat and mixed with the liquid in that.

Monsteraun said, "his quest is complete", and started to struggle. Everyone's heart started pounding very hard.

Draco took off his head, there was no head left now. Everyone was startled on seeing that. He blew fire on it through his windpipe. The beasts fell on the ground and struggled, including Draco.

Monsteraun started to struggle even more, soon, his struggling stopped, it was a sign that, the quest was complete. Volinoir fell on his knees and burst out in tears. Everyone started crying.

Outside, the soldiers who were fighting got surprised on seeing that all the dark soldiers had disappeared. But when they realized their king has died, they all also burst out into tears.

It was completed. His quest!

Epilogue

The legend of King Ultimox Draco and his 7 beasts continued for generations and fascinated every single person who heard of this. After the death of King Ultimox Draco, they completed his dying wish of donating every single coin of the royal treasury.

Drake didn't have any reason to be at Sedcas anymore so he was sent back to earth, where his step parents were waiting for him. They didn't abuse him a lot after this.

Dorgard didn't have any work to do, so he retired and lived in his own house with his family.

He still did a little bit investigation to find the bodies of the dead, but he didn't find. Legend has it that their bodies evaporated into the heavens. Maybe they really did.

King Volinoir Draco had died after a few days the death of his son. As he left no heirs to become the king, the great Draco Dynasty had come to an end. It's true; it was not such a great idea to make little kids kings. They have just come to the world and you give them to rule it? Well, we end the way we begun. It's true, Kings are not born, they are made.

ABOUT THE AUTHOR

Syed Shehzor Mujthedi was born in India, on 25th April 2002. He studied in Jubilee Hills Public School. He was interested in writing since he was a child. When he was in first grade, he would make comic strips on rough pages.

He loved to write comic books but later, his ambition changed from comics to novels. He started writing his first novel, the 7 beasts at the age of 9. He liked to read comics and encyclopedias but mainly focuses on classic novels these days.

In his childhood, he had written many novels as a part of hobby. Some of his novels were The Ghost of The Barber, Beethoven and Bane, The Tremendous Train Teamers, etc.

At the age of 11, he found this website called wattpad. It was an e book writing website. He wrote many stories in it as well. He published his first novel, The 7 Beasts in 2014. He is looking forward to publish more books.